A NEWBERY HALLOWEEN

Also selected by
Martin H. Greenberg and Charles G. Waugh:

A Newbery Christmas:
Fourteen stories of Christmas by
Newbery Award–winning authors

A NEWBERY HALLOWEEN

*A dozen
scary stories
by Newbery Award–winning
authors*

Selected by
Martin H. Greenberg
and
Charles G. Waugh

Introduction by Lloyd Alexander

DELACORTE PRESS/NEW YORK

Published by Delacorte Press
Bantam Doubleday Dell Publishing Group, Inc.
1540 Broadway, New York, New York 10036

Acknowledgments

"The Baddest Witch in the World" by Beverly Cleary—From RAMONA THE PEST by Beverly Cleary. Copyright © 1968 by Beverly Cleary. By permission of Morrow Junior Books, a division of William Morrow & Co., Inc.

"Witch Girl" by Elizabeth Coatsworth—Copyright 1953 by *Story Parade*. Reprinted by permission of Kate Barnes for the Estate of Elizabeth Coatsworth.

"A Halloween to Remember" by E. L. Konigsburg—Reprinted with the permission of Atheneum Publishers, an imprint of Macmillan Publishing Company from JENNIFER, HECATE, MACBETH, WILLIAM MCKINLEY, AND ME, ELIZABETH (Chapters 1 & 2) by E. L. Konigsburg. Copyright © 1967 by E. L. Konigsburg.

"The Ghost in the Attic" by Eleanor Estes—From THE MOFFATS by Eleanor Estes, copyright 1941 by Harcourt Brace & Company and renewed 1969 by Eleanor Estes, reprinted by permission of the publisher.

"Poor Little Saturday" by Madeleine L'Engle—Copyright © 1956 by King-Size Publications. Reprinted by permission of Lescher & Lescher, Ltd.

"Ah Tcha the Sleeper" by Arthur Bowie Chrisman—From SHEN OF THE SEA by Arthur Bowie Chrisman. Copyright 1952 by E. P. Dutton, renewed 1953 by Arthur Bowie Chrisman. Used by permission of Dutton's Children's Books, a division of Penguin Books USA Inc.

"The Witch's Eye" by Phyllis Reynolds Naylor—An extract, as approved by Phyllis Reynolds Naylor, from her THE WITCH'S EYE. Copyright © 1990 by Phyllis Reynolds Naylor. By permission of Delacorte Press, a division of Bantam Doubleday Dell Publishing Group, Inc.

"The Magic Ball" by Charles J. Finger—From TALES FROM SILVER LANDS by Charles J. Finger. Copyright 1924 by Doubleday, a division of Bantam Doubleday Dell Publishing Group, Inc. Used by permission of Doubleday, a division of Bantam Doubleday Dell Publishing Group, Inc.

"The Man of Influence" by Paul Fleischman—From GRAVEN IMAGES by Paul Fleischman. Copyright © 1982 by Paul Fleischman. HarperCollins Publishers, Inc.

"Camp Fat" by E. L. Konigsburg—Reprinted with the permission of Atheneum Publishers, an imprint of Macmillan Publishing Company from ALTOGETHER, ONE AT A TIME by E. L. Konigsburg. Copyright © 1971 by E. L. Konigsburg.

"The Horse of the War God" by Elizabeth Coatsworth—Copyright 1932 by Elizabeth Coatsworth. From CRICKET AND THE EMPEROR'S SON by Elizabeth Coatsworth. Reprinted by permission of Kate Barnes for the Estate of Elizabeth Coatsworth.

"The Year Halloween Happened One Day Early" by Virginia Hamilton—An extract, as approved by Virginia Hamilton, from her WILLIE BEA AND THE TIME THE MARTIANS LANDED. Copyright © 1983 by Virginia Hamilton Adoff. By permission of Greenwillow Books, a division of William Morrow & Company, Inc.

Library of Congress Cataloging in Publication Data

A Newbery Halloween : twelve scary stories by Newbery award-winning authors / selected by Martin H. Greenberg and Charles G. Waugh.
    p. cm.
    Summary: A collection of short stories with a Halloween theme, by such Newbery Award-winning authors as E. L. Konigsburg, Beverly Cleary, Virginia Hamilton, and Paul Fleischman.
    ISBN 0-385-31028-5
    1. Halloween—Juvenile fiction. 2. Children's stories, American. [1. Halloween—Fiction. 2. Short stories.] I. Greenberg, Martin Harry. II. Waugh, Charles.
PZ5.N395 1993
[Fic]—dc20   92-43877   CIP   AC

Manufactured in the United States of America

September 1993

10 9 8 7 6 5 4 3 2 1

MVA

TABLE OF CONTENTS

Contents

Lloyd Alexander

INTRODUCTION

THE ASSORTMENT OF ghosts, witches, and various pranksters are gathered here for a common purpose: to scare the wits out of us—deliciously; to make us shiver and shriek; and, above all, to delight us. They do it fiendishly well too. And no wonder. For, under the masks and costumes, they're among our most artful storytellers; indeed, a very distinguished company of Newbery Medalists.

The trick-or-treaters knocking at the door and rattling the windows aren't all youngsters. Parents and grandparents will be happy to see some of their own childhood favorites, such as Elizabeth Coatsworth and Eleanor Estes. It's a special pleasure to be reminded of Charles J. Finger, whose contribution is one of the few and surely one of the finest supernatural tales with a Latin-American setting; and Arthur Bowie Chrisman's beautifully told Chinese story.

Young readers will recognize and eagerly welcome their best-loved authors and characters. No Halloween party, for example, would be complete without the shenanigans of Ramona the Pest, from Beverly Cleary; and E. L. Konigsburg's Jennifer. Madeleine L'Engle magically whisks us away to South Georgia and a remarkable witch woman. Phyllis Reynolds Naylor haunts us with a witch's evil eye. Virginia Hamilton evokes the notorious 1938 hoax by Orson Welles that convinced a panicky United States that Martians had landed in New Jersey. In an entirely different mood, with an Italian baroque flavor, Paul Fleischman serves up terror in the grand manner.

In sum, this sack of Halloween goodies includes everything from mythic to modern, from unearthly fantasy to down-to-earth realism, and readers will savor each one.

The genial hosts (not ghosts) and guiding spirits in the festivities are Martin H. Greenberg and Charles G. Waugh. They've made their selections with an unerring eye—and ear, for the stories are splendid read-alouds for young people and their elders. Anywhere, anytime. A *Newbery Halloween* goes well beyond the ordinary seasonal collection and genre tale.

Yes, of course, this present volume is fun, with chills, thrills, and bursts of laughter. As well, there are bright strands of beauty, poetry, and moments of unexpected poignancy. It's a very durable collection, reaching past the Halloween season, which is short, to enrich young readers' literary experiences, which is a lifelong process.

As for tricks and treats, there are plenty. These Newbery laureates give us both.

A NEWBERY HALLOWEEN

Beverly Cleary

THE BADDEST WITCH
IN THE WORLD

WHEN THE MORNING kindergarten cut jack-o'-lanterns from orange paper and pasted them on the windows so that the light shone through the eye and mouth holes, Ramona knew that at last Halloween was not far away. Next to Christmas and her birthday, Ramona liked Halloween best. She liked dressing up and going trick-or-treating after dark with Beezus. She liked those nights when the bare branches of trees waved against the streetlights, and the world was a ghostly place. Ramona liked scaring people, and she liked the shivery feeling of being scared herself.

Ramona had always enjoyed going to school with her mother to watch the boys and girls of Glenwood School parade on the playground in their Halloween costumes. Afterward she used to eat a doughnut and drink a paper cup of apple juice if there happened to be some left over. This year, after years of sitting on the benches with mothers and little brothers and sisters, Ramona was finally going to get to wear a costume and march around and around the playground. This year she had a doughnut and apple juice coming to her.

"Mama, did you buy my mask?" Ramona asked every day, when she came home from school.

"Not today, dear," Mrs. Quimby answered. "Don't pester. I'll get it the next time I go down to the shopping center."

Ramona, who did not mean to pester her mother, could not see why grownups had to be so slow. "Make it a bad mask, Mama," she said. "I want to be the baddest witch in the whole world."

"You mean the worst witch," Beezus said, whenever she happened to overhear this conversation.

"I do not," contradicted Ramona. "I mean the baddest witch." "Baddest witch" sounded much scarier than "worst witch," and Ramona did enjoy stories about bad witches, the badder the better. She had no patience with books about good witches, because witches were supposed to be bad. Ramona had chosen to be a witch for that very reason.

Then one day when Ramona came home from school she found two paper bags on the foot of her bed. One contained black material and a pattern for a witch costume. The picture on the pattern showed the witch's hat pointed like the letter A. Ramona reached into the second bag and pulled out a rubber witch mask so scary that she quickly dropped it on the bed because she was not sure she even wanted to touch it.

The flabby thing was the grayish-green color of mold and had stringy hair, a hooked nose, snaggle teeth, and a wart on its nose. Its empty eyes seemed to stare at Ramona with a look of evil. The face was so ghastly that Ramona had to remind herself that it was only a rubber mask from the dime store before she could summon enough courage to pick it up and slip it over her head.

Ramona peeked cautiously in the mirror, backed away, and then gathered her courage for a longer look. That's really me in there, she told herself and felt better. She ran off to show her mother and discovered that she felt very brave when she was inside the mask and did not have to look at it. "I'm the baddest witch in the world!" she shouted, her voice muffled by the mask, and was delighted when her mother was so frightened she dropped her sewing.

Ramona waited for Beezus and her father to come home, so she could put on her mask and jump out and scare them. But that night, before she went to bed, she rolled up the mask and hid it behind a cushion of the couch in the living room.

"What are you doing that for?" asked Beezus, who had nothing to be afraid of. She was planning to be a princess and wear a narrow pink mask.

"Because I want to," answered Ramona, who did not care to sleep in the same room with that ghastly, leering face.

Afterward when Ramona wanted to frighten herself she would lift the cushion for a quick glimpse of her scary mask before she clapped the pillow over it again. Scaring herself was such fun.

When Ramona's costume was finished and the day of the Halloween parade arrived, the morning kindergarten had trouble sitting still for seat work. They wiggled so much while resting on their mats that Miss Binney had to wait a long time before she found someone quiet enough to be the wake-up fairy. When kindergarten was finally dismissed, the whole class forgot the rules and went stampeding out the door. At home Ramona ate only the soft part of her tuna-fish sandwich, because her mother insisted she could not go to the Halloween parade on an empty stomach. She wadded the crusts into her paper napkin and hid them beneath the edge of her plate before she ran to her room to put on her long black dress, her cape, her mask, and her pointed witch hat held on by an elastic under her chin. Ramona had doubts about that elastic—none of the witches whom she met in books seemed to have elastic under their chin—but today she was too happy and excited to bother to make a fuss.

"See, Mama!" she cried. "I'm the baddest witch in the world!"

Mrs. Quimby smiled at Ramona, patted her through the long black dress, and said affectionately, "Sometimes I think you are."

"Come on, Mama! Let's go to the Halloween parade." Ramona had waited so long that she did not see how she could wait another five minutes.

"I told Howie's mother we would wait for them," said Mrs. Quimby.

"Mama, did you have to?" protested Ramona, running to the front window to watch for Howie. Fortunately, Mrs. Kemp and Willa Jean were already approaching with Howie dressed in a black cat costume lagging along behind, holding the end of his tail in one hand. Willa Jean in her stroller was wearing a buck-toothed rabbit mask.

Ramona could not wait. She burst out the front door yelling through her mask, "Yah! Yah! I'm the baddest witch in the world! Hurry, Howie! I'm going to get you, Howie!"

Howie walked stolidly along, lugging his tail, so Ramona ran out to meet him. He was not wearing a mask, but instead had pipe cleaners Scotch-taped to his face for whiskers.

"I'm the baddest witch in the world," Ramona informed him, "and you can be my cat."

"I don't want to be your cat," said Howie. "I don't want to be a cat at all."

"Why not, Howie?" asked Mrs. Quimby, who had joined Ramona and the Kemps. "I think you make a very nice cat."

"My tail is busted," complained Howie. "I don't want to be a cat with a busted tail."

Mrs. Kemp sighed. "Now, Howie, if you'll just hold up the end of your tail nobody will notice." Then she said to Mrs. Quimby, "I promised him a pirate costume, but his older sister was sick and while I was taking her temperature Willa Jean crawled into a cupboard and managed to dump a whole quart of salad oil all over the kitchen floor. If you've ever had to clean oil off a floor, you know what I went through, and then Howie went into the bathroom and climbed up—yes, dear, I understand you wanted to help—to get a sponge, and he accidentally knelt on a tube of toothpaste that someone had left the top off of—now, Howie, I didn't say you left the top off—and toothpaste squirted all over the bathroom, and there was another mess to clean up. Well, I finally had to drag his sister's old cat costume out of a drawer, and when he put it on we discovered the wire in the tail was broken, but there wasn't time to rip it apart and put in a new wire."

"You have a handsome set of whiskers," said Mrs. Quimby, trying to coax Howie to look on the bright side.

"Scotch tape itches me," said Howie.

Ramona could see that Howie was not going to be any fun at all, even on Halloween. Never mind. She would have fun all by herself. "I'm the baddest witch in the world," she sang in her muffled voice, skipping with both feet. "I'm the baddest witch in the world."

When they were in sight of the playground, Ramona saw that it was already swarming with both the morning and the afternoon kindergartens in their Halloween costumes. Poor Miss Binney, dressed like Mother Goose, now had the responsibility of sixty-eight boys and girls. "Run along, Ramona," said Mrs. Quimby, when they had crossed the street. "Howie's mother and I will go around to the big playground and try to find a seat on a bench before they are all taken."

Ramona ran screaming onto the playground. "Yah! Yah! I'm the baddest witch in the world!" Nobody paid any attention, because everyone else was screaming, too. The noise was glorious. Ramona yelled and screamed and shrieked and chased anyone who would run. She chased tramps and ghosts and ballerinas. Sometimes other witches in masks exactly like hers chased her, and then she would turn around and chase the witches right back. She tried to chase Howie, but he would not run. He just stood beside the fence holding his broken tail and missing all the fun.

Ramona discovered dear little Davy in a skimpy pirate

costume from the dime store. She could tell he was Davy by his thin legs. At last! She pounced and kissed him through her rubber mask. Davy looked startled, but he had the presence of mind to make a gagging noise while Ramona raced away, satisfied that she finally had managed to catch and kiss Davy.

Then Ramona saw Susan getting out of her mother's car. As she might have guessed, Susan was dressed as an old-fashioned girl with a long skirt, an apron, and pantalettes. "I'm the baddest witch in the world!" yelled Ramona, and ran after Susan whose curls bobbed daintily about her shoulders in a way that could not be disguised. Ramona was unable to resist. After weeks of longing she tweaked one of Susan's curls, and yelled, *"Boing!"* through her rubber mask.

"You stop that," said Susan, and smoothed her curls.

"Yah! Yah! I'm the baddest witch in the world!" Ramona was carried away. She tweaked another curl and yelled a muffled, *"Boing!"*

A clown laughed and joined Ramona. He too tweaked a curl and yelled, *"Boing!"*

The old-fashioned girl stamped her foot. "You stop that!" she said angrily.

"Boing! Boing!" Others joined the game. Susan tried to run away, but no matter which way she ran there was someone eager to stretch a curl and yell, *"Boing!"* Susan ran to Miss Binney. "Miss Binney! Miss Binney!" she cried. "They're teasing me! They're pulling my hair and boinging me!"

"Who's teasing you?" asked Miss Binney.

"Everybody," said Susan tearfully. "A witch started it."

"Which witch?" asked Miss Binney.

Susan looked around. "I don't know, which witch," she said, "but it was a bad witch."

That's me, the baddest witch in the world, thought Ramona. At the same time she was a little surprised. That others really would not know that she was behind her mask had never occurred to her.

"Never mind, Susan," said Miss Binney. "You stay near me, and no one will tease you."

Which witch, thought Ramona, liking the sound of the words. Which witch, which witch. As the words ran through her thoughts Ramona began to wonder if Miss Binney could guess who she was. She ran up to her teacher and shouted in her muffled voice, "Hello, Miss Binney! I'm going to get you, Miss Binney!"

"Ooh, what a scary witch!" said Miss Binney, rather absentmindedly, Ramona thought. Plainly Miss Binney was not really frightened, and with so many witches running around she had not recognized Ramona.

No, Miss Binney was not the one who was frightened. Ramona was. Miss Binney did not know who this witch was. Nobody knew who Ramona was, and if nobody knew who she was, she wasn't anybody.

"Get out of the way, old witch!" Eric R. yelled at Ramona. He did not say, Get out of the way, Ramona.

Ramona could not remember a time when there was not someone near who knew who she was. Even last Halloween, when she dressed up as a ghost and went trick-or-treating with Beezus and the older boys and girls, everyone seemed to know who she was. "I can guess who this little ghost is," the neighbors said, as they dropped a miniature candy bar or a handful of peanuts into her paper bag. And now, with so many witches running around and still more witches on the big playground, no one knew who she was.

"Davy, guess who I am!" yelled Ramona. Surely Davy would know.

"You're just another old witch," answered Davy.

The feeling was the scariest one Ramona had ever experienced. She felt lost inside her costume. She wondered if her mother would know which witch was which, and the thought that her own mother might not know her frightened Ramona even more. What if her mother forgot her? What if everyone in the whole world forgot her? With that terrifying thought Ramona snatched off her mask, and although its ugliness was no longer the most frightening thing about it, she rolled it up so she would not have to look at it.

How cool the air felt outside that dreadful mask! Ramona no longer wanted to be the baddest witch in the world. She wanted to be Ramona Geraldine Quimby and be sure that Miss Binney and everyone on the playground knew her. Around her the ghosts and tramps and pirates raced and shouted, but Ramona stood near the door of the kindergarten quietly watching.

Davy raced up to her and yelled. "Yah! You can't catch me!"

"I don't want to catch you," Ramona informed him.

Davy looked surprised and a little disappointed, but he ran off on his thin little legs, shouting, "Yo-ho-ho and a bottle of rum!"

Joey yelled after him, "You're not really a pirate. You're just Mush Pot Davy!"

Miss Binney was trying to herd her sixty-eight charges into a double line. Two mothers who felt sorry for the teacher were helping round up the kindergarten to start the Halloween parade, but as always there were some children who would rather run around than do what they were supposed to do. For once Ramona was not one of them. On the big playground someone started to play a marching record through a loudspeaker. The Halloween parade that Ramona had looked forward to since she was in nursery school was about to begin.

"Come along, children," said Miss Binney. Seeing Ramona standing alone, she said, "Come on, Ramona."

It was a great relief to Ramona to hear Miss Binney speak her name, to hear her teacher say "Ramona" when she was looking at her. But as much as Ramona longed to prance along to the marching music with the rest of her class, she did not move to join them.

"Put on your mask, Ramona, and get in line," said Miss Binney, guiding a ghost and a gypsy into place.

Ramona wanted to obey her teacher, but at the same time she was afraid of losing herself behind that scary mask. The line of kindergartners, all of them wearing masks except Howie with his pipe-cleaner whiskers, was less straggly now, and everyone was eager to start the parade. If Ramona did not do something quickly she would be left behind, and she could not let such a thing happen, not when she had waited so many years to be in a Halloween parade.

Ramona took only a moment to decide what to do. She ran to her cupboard inside the kindergarten building and snatched a crayon from her box. Then she grabbed a piece of paper from the supply cupboard. Outside she could hear the many feet of the morning and afternoon kindergartens marching off to the big playground. There was no time for Ramona's best printing, but that was all right. This job was not seat work to be supervised by Miss Binney. As fast as she could Ramona printed her name, and then she could not resist adding with a flourish her last initial complete with ears and whiskers.

RAMONA Q

Now the whole world would know who she was! She was Ramona Quimby, the only girl in the world with ears and whiskers on her last initial. Ramona pulled on her rubber mask, clapped her pointed hat on top of it, snapped the elastic under her chin, and ran after her class as it marched onto the big playground. She did not care if she was last in line and had to march beside gloomy old Howie still lugging his broken tail.

Around the playground marched the kindergarten followed by the first grade and all the other grades while mothers and little brothers and sisters watched. Ramona felt very grown-up remembering how last year she had been a little sister sitting on a bench watching for her big sister, Beezus, to march by and hoping for a leftover doughnut.

"Yah! Yah! I'm the baddest witch in the world!" Ramona chanted, as she held up her sign for all to see. Around the playground she marched toward her mother, who was waiting on the bench. Her mother saw her, pointed her out to Mrs. Kemp, and waved. Ramona beamed inside her stuffy mask. Her mother recognized her!

Poor little Willa Jean in her stroller could not read, so

Ramona called out to her, "It's me, Willa Jean. I'm Ramona, the baddest witch in the world!"

Willa Jean in her rabbit mask understood. She laughed and slapped her hands on the tray of her stroller.

Ramona saw Henry's dog, Ribsy, trotting along, supervising the parade. "Yah! Ribsy! I'm going to get you, Ribsy!" she threatened, as she marched past.

Ribsy gave a short bark, and Ramona was sure that even Ribsy knew who she was as she marched off to collect her doughnut and apple juice.

(Note: "The Baddest Witch in the World" is taken from Chapter 6 of *Ramona the Pest*.)

Elizabeth Coatsworth

WITCH GIRL

IT WAS A WINDY autumn night with clouds blowing across the stars. Slowly and wearily five travelers moved down the moorland road.

"Aren't we ever coming to a house, Uncle Philip?" the little girl asked, trying to stifle a sob.

"Patience, Ann," said the young man.

Her father, at the head of the little procession, was leading the old white plow-horse on which his wife rode with the youngest child in her arms. Now, he said bitterly, "The people at the last inn told us that we should come to shelter long before this."

Suddenly the little girl came closer to her uncle.

"What was that?" she asked in terror.

"It sounded like a dog howling."

"Or a wolf," her father mumbled.

Philip stooped down and picked up Ann in his arms. "I'll carry you now."

Without halting, they went on, even though the white horse pulled back at the bit and began to sweat and shake.

Suddenly the horse shied. Out of the shadows a figure appeared, walking toward them. Unnoticed, the moon had risen. Now there was light enough for the travelers to see that the newcomer was a young girl in a dark cloak, with dark hair blowing about her face.

She seemed to be out of breath.

"We heard you coming," she said. "My grandmother, my two aunts—we live in a little house, only a mile from here. They are making everything ready for you."

"How kind!" the woman on the horse exclaimed. "And for you to have run to meet us, too! What is your name, my dear?"

The girl hesitated for a moment. "They call me Pretty," she said.

"An unusual name," said the woman, "but it suits you. Do let us go on, John. Poor Whitey is so tired that he shivers all the time."

"Walk with us," said Philip to the girl. "Whitey seems afraid of everything tonight, and you're a stranger, but if you're back here he won't see you."

The girl fell into step beside him, and their eyes met in the moonlight.

"You look tired," said Pretty. "Let me carry the little girl."

"No, I'm all right. Ann's too heavy for you."

The child buried her face in her uncle's shoulder. She seemed afraid.

The little boy in his mother's arms woke with a cry.

"What's the matter, darling?"

"Crows were pecking at my face, Mother."

"That was only a bad dream, dear. Soon we are going to be safe in a house," his mother soothed him. Only she seemed to be entirely unafraid.

Something passed overhead.

"What was that?" Philip asked.

"Only my—" Pretty broke off. "Only a bird."

"It looked very queer and long, almost like a broom."

"The moonlight plays strange tricks. It must have been a night heron with a long bill."

"Yes," said Philip. "It must have been a heron." And they walked on again.

The woman on the white horse began singing a lullaby, her head bent over the drowsing child. The others walked on in silence. Now and then Whitey snorted, as though still afraid.

Over the long moor they saw lighted windows, still far off.

"Now we shall be all right," said the woman. "How good you have been to help us, Pretty."

"I am *not* good," said Pretty, twisting her hands. "My real name is Pretty Spella, and I am learning to be a witch." Her eyes looked frightened.

"A witch!" everyone exclaimed.

"I'm not much good as a witch," Pretty confessed. "I

don't like mixing the brews or making spells to hurt people. But they're raising me to be a witch just the same."

"I'm sure you're a dear, good girl," said the young woman. "If you're in trouble, perhaps we can help you."

"Oh, thank you," said Pretty. She hesitated, and then her words came in a breathless rush.

"I was an orphan and the fat witch called Horrible took me when I was little and has brought me up. She's good to me in her way, but Hag-Chaser hates me because I won't pat Hop-in-the-Fire, her toad. She wants to turn *me* into a toad."

"Mercy me!" said the young mother, and Philip exclaimed suddenly, "We'll take care of you."

"At least forewarned is forearmed," said Ann's father. "Now this young lady had better tell us what we can do to save ourselves, if she knows."

"I know some things about spells, but not everything," said Pretty, who spoke with more confidence since everyone was acting in such a friendly manner.

"In the first place, the house you will see isn't a *real* house. It's made from a square of thistles, bewitched. And the three witches won't look like themselves at all, but like nice country women. Even Grimalkin will have a ribbon around her neck."

Pretty went on telling all she knew with her face very white and earnest in the moonlight, and her eyes very large and bright, and her hair softer than shadows.

"Don't let the children out of your sight for a moment," Pretty warned them. "Whoever eats a single crumb will be in their power. Remember, neither sip nor sup. But if you don't stop at the cottage, they'll send wolves to pursue you, or surround you with fire, or some other awful sorcery. And while you are talking, I will try to find the spell book. It takes different shapes, sometimes large, sometimes small, but it is always oblong. They can't any of them make spells without it. Our only hope lies in destroying the book, and then they will be powerless, and you can escape."

"Yes," said Philip, "and when we leave, Pretty will come with us. And I am going to marry her."

Pretty didn't say yes, and Pretty didn't say no, but in the darkness she flushed as red as a rose. But only Philip noticed.

"We must go on," said the woman on the horse. "They'll be waiting. John, take Ann, and let Philip and Pretty lead Whitey. Everything will be all right."

They were met at the cottage door by three nice-looking old ladies in fresh dresses of sprigged calico. One old lady was rather fat, and one old lady was rather small, and the third old lady was tall as a maypole. But what of that?

There was a black cat by the hearth asleep on a cushion, and the brooms in the corner behind the door gave a rattle all by themselves when the strangers came in. But what of that? If the fire seemed to talk to itself, and the teakettle whistled like a blackbird, and a big toad hopped hastily off the step as they approached: these things might happen anywhere.

Whitey, who appeared too frightened to whinny, was fastened to the hitching post by the door, and the travelers all went into the low room, bright with candles and warm with fire.

And how the three old ladies welcomed the newcomers!

How they helped them off with their cloaks and brought out chairs by the fire for them! How they admired the beautiful children!

"You must be hungry," said the fat old lady.

"Oh, no, thank you. We have eaten," said the young mother, smiling.

The little white-haired lady, no larger than a six-year-old child, climbed onto a stool and got a plate heaped with cookies and tarts from the shelf.

"Now, I know you'll all want some of my sweets," she said. "There are blackberry tarts and blueberry cookies, and the little ones are sprinkled with black walnuts. Take your pick, my bird," she said to the little boy on his mother's lap.

But his mother gently pulled back his hand. "Eating at night gives him bad dreams," she said.

"But you're too old to dream, aren't you, Honeysuckle?" said the little lady, sliding close to Ann, who stood by the fire.

"No, thank you, ma'am," said Ann, looking wistfully at the tarts.

"It's good manners to take one, child!"

"Shall I, Father?" asked Ann.

Her father shook his head. "Eating at night doesn't agree with Ann either."

"Look out!" exclaimed the cat.

The three old ladies immediately stopped what they were doing and looked about the room wildly. There was Pretty in a corner reaching toward a cobweb overhead, on which sat a black, rather oblong-looking spider.

"Let that alone!" shrieked Horrible, waving her arms at Pretty Spella.

"Stop! Stop," shrilled little Scrits.

It was Hag-Chaser who gave a thin, long leap across the room toward the girl, reaching out with her clutching fingers.

Philip stepped in front of Pretty with his staff raised. "Keep back!" he cried.

"Brooms! Brooms! Help!" shrieked the three old ladies together, and instantly three brooms hopped from behind the door and made for Philip and the girl immediately and with great speed. But swifter still, a fourth broom with a red handle came hurrying up from another corner and barred their path.

While the young mother clutched her little boy, and John picked up Ann and carried her out of the way, the battle raged. The old ladies shrieked and the brooms fought, handle clashing against handle. Philip joined the defense of the red broomstick against the others, while the cat yowled and bit his ankle, and the toad came huffing and puffing through a hole in the wainscot.

But Pretty had seized the spider, web and all, and still protected by Philip and the red-handled broom, she gained the hearth and flung the oblong-shaped creature into the flames.

Instantly the fire leaped up into the chimney throat, the brooms fell with a clatter to the floor, and the candles winked low and rose again. Hop-in-the-Fire huffed and puffed back through the hole, Grimalkin returned to her cushion, and the three old ladies began to set their aprons straight, and fluff up the ribbons of their white caps.

"Oh deary me," whimpered little Scrits. "What will become of us now?"

"No one will fear us," mumbled the fat witch called Horrible.

"We'll starve," moaned Hag-Chaser.

The young mother looked troubled. "Can't you just go on living here?" she said. "It's such a nice cottage."

"But how are we to maintain ourselves, Madam?" said Horrible, crossly.

"Couldn't you weave?"

"I used to weave cloth before I wove spells," said Hag-Chaser unexpectedly, "and Scrits made rag rugs very nicely, long ago when she was young."

"My specialty was linen. That, too, was long ago," added Horrible, "but I still remember."

The three old ladies became quite enthusiastic as they talked.

"It will be a change," said Scrits. "Anything for a change. And we're very near the road. We should get good trade."

"I will send you my cookbook, and you will find it much more fun than a spell book, I know," said the young mother.

"How kind you are, Madam!" exclaimed little Scrits, making an effort to smile. "And now you'd better all be getting on. The village is only a mile beyond us. You go too, Pretty Spella, with your fine young man by your side!"

"Yes, good-bye," said Hag-Chaser. "I always said you'd be our ruin, girl."

"You weren't cut out for a witch, ever," said Horrible kindly. "This new form of life will fit you better, so run along, my dear."

The travelers were glad enough to go. No sip nor sup had

they taken. Whitey, too, was glad to leave the little cottage behind. And Pretty walked with her young man's arm about her, carrying with her the faithful broom with the red handle.

"Oh, not for riding of course," she assured Philip. "I'm done with all that, and the poor thing is only an ordinary broom now, anyway. But we did have some wonderful rides together. It's not wrong for me to remember them, is it?"

"Certainly not," said Philip. "What a good fight it put up tonight! I shall buy a silver hook for it, and it shall hang on our kitchen wall in the place of honor when we are married."

E. L. Konigsburg

A HALLOWEEN TO
REMEMBER

I FIRST MET JENNIFER on my way to school. It was Halloween, and she was sitting in a tree. I was going back to school from lunch. This particular lunch hour was only a little different from usual because of Halloween. We were told to dress in costume for the school Halloween parade. I was dressed as a Pilgrim.

I always walked the back road to school, and I always walked alone. We had moved to the apartment house in town in September just before school started, and I walked alone because I didn't have anyone to walk with. I walked the back way because it passed through a little woods that I liked. Jennifer was sitting in one of the trees in this woods.

Our apartment house had grown on a farm about ten

years before. There was still a small farm across the street; it included a big white house, a greenhouse, a caretaker's house, and a pump painted green without a handle. The greenhouse had clean windows; they shone in the sun. I could see only the roof windows from our second floor apartment. The rest were hidden by trees and shrubs. My mother never called the place a farm; she always called it THE ESTATE. It was old; the lady who owned it was old. She had given part of her land to the town for a park, and the town named the park after her: Samellson Park. THE ESTATE gave us a beautiful view from our apartment. My mother liked trees.

Our new town was not full of apartments. Almost everyone else lived in houses. There were only three apartment buildings as big as ours. All three sat on the top of the hill from the train station. Hundreds of men rode the train to New York City every morning and rode it home every night. My father did. In the mornings the elevators would be full of kids going to school and fathers going to the train. The kids left the building by the back door and ran down one side of the hill to the school. The fathers left the building by the front door and ran down the other side of the hill to the station.

Other kids from the apartment chose to walk to school through the little woods. The footsteps of all of them for ten years had worn away the soil so that the roots of the trees were bare and made steps for walking up and down the steep slope. The little woods made better company than the sidewalks. I liked the smells of the trees and the colors of the trees. I liked to walk with my head way up, practically hanging over my back. Then I could see the patterns the leaves formed against the blue sky.

I had my head way back and was watching the leaves when I first saw Jennifer up in the tree. She was dressed as a Pilgrim, too. I saw her feet first. She was sitting on one of the lower branches of the tree swinging her feet. That's how I happened to see her feet first. They were just about the boniest feet I had ever seen. Swinging right in front of my eyes as if I were sitting in the first row at Cinerama. They wore real Pilgrim shoes made of buckles and cracked old leather. The heel part flapped up and down because the shoes were so big that only the toe part could stay attached. Those shoes looked as if they were going to fall off any minute.

I grabbed the heel of the shoe and shoved it back onto the heel of that bony foot. Then I wiped my hands on my Pilgrim apron and looked up at Jennifer. I didn't know yet that she was Jennifer. She was not smiling, and I was embarrassed.

I said in a loud voice, which I hoped would sound stout red but which came out sounding thin blue, "You're going to lose that shoe."

The first thing Jennifer ever said to me was, "Witches never lose anything."

"But you're not a witch," I said. "You're a Pilgrim, and look, so am I."

"I won't argue with you," she said. "Witches convince; they never argue. But I'll tell you this much. Real witches are Pilgrims, and just because I don't have on a silly black costume and carry a silly broom and wear a silly black hat, doesn't mean that I'm not a witch. I'm a witch all the time and not just on Halloween."

I didn't know what to say, so I said what my mother always says when she can't answer one of my questions. I said, "You better hurry up now, or you'll be late for school."

"Witches are never late," she said.

"But witches have to go to school." I wished I had said something clever.

"I just go to school because I'm putting the teacher under a spell," she said.

"Which teacher?" I asked. "Get it? *Witch* teacher?" I laughed. I was pleased that now I had said something clever.

Jennifer neither laughed nor answered. But I was sure she'd got it. She looked at me hard and said, "Give me those three chocolate chip cookies, and I'll come down and tell you my name, and I'll walk the rest of the way to school with you."

I wasn't particularly hungry for the cookies, but I was hungry for company, so I said, "Okay," and reached out my hand holding the cookies. I wondered how she could tell that they were chocolate chips. They were in a bag.

As she began to swing down from the branches, I caught a glimpse of her underwear. I expected that it would look dusty, and it did. But that was not why it was not like any underwear I had ever seen. It was old fashioned. There were buttons and no elastic. She also had on yards and yards of petticoats. Her Pilgrim dress looked older than mine. Much older. Much, much older. Hers looked ancient. Of course, my Pilgrim costume was not new either. I had worn it the year before, but then I had been in a different grade in a different school. My cousin had worn the costume before that. I hadn't grown much during the year. My dress was only a little short, and only a little tight, and only a little scratchy where it was pinned, and it was only absolutely uncomfortable. In other words, my costume was a hand-me-down, but Jennifer's was a genuine antique.

After Jennifer touched the ground, I saw that she was taller than I. Everybody was. I was the shortest kid in my class. I was always the shortest kid in my class. She was thin. Skinny is what she really was. She came toward my hand and looked hard at the bag of cookies.

"Are you sure you didn't bite any of them?" she demanded.

"Sure I'm sure," I said. I was getting mad, but a bargain's a bargain.

"Well," she said, taking one cookie out of the bag, "my name is Jennifer. Now let's get going." As she said "going," she grabbed the bag with the other two cookies and started to walk.

"Wait up," I yelled. "A bargain's a bargain. Don't you want to know my name?"

"I told you witches are never late, but I can't be responsible for you yet . . . Elizabeth."

She knew my name already! She walked so fast that I was almost convinced that she was a witch; she was practically flying. We got to school just as the tardy bell began to ring. Jennifer's room was a fifth grade just off the corridor near the entrance, and she slipped into her classroom while the bell was still buzzing. My room was four doors further down the hall, and I got to my room *after* the bell had stopped.

She had said that witches are never late. Being late felt as uncomfortable as my tight Pilgrim dress. No Pilgrim had ever suffered as much as I did. Walking to my seat while everyone stared at me was awful. My desk was in the back of the room; it was a long, long walk. The whole class had time to see that I was a blushing Pilgrim. I knew that I was ready to cry. The whole class didn't have to know that too, so I didn't raise my eyes until I was seated and felt sure that they wouldn't leak. When I looked up, I saw that there were six Pilgrims: three other Pilgrim girls and two Pilgrim boys. That's a lot of Pilgrims for a class of twenty. But none of them could be witches, I thought. After checking over their costumes and shoes, I decided that at least three of them had cousins who had been Pilgrims the year before.

Miss Hazen announced that she would postpone my detention until the next day because of the Halloween parade. Detention was a school rule; if you were late coming to school, you stayed after school that day. The kids called it "staying after." I didn't feel grateful for the postponement. She could have skipped my "staying after" altogether.

Our lesson that afternoon was short, and I didn't perform too well. I had to tug on my dress a lot and scratch under my Pilgrim hat a lot. I would have scratched other places where the costume itched, but they weren't polite.

At last we were all lined up in the hall. Each class was to march to the auditorium and be seated. Then one class at a time would walk across the stage before the judges. The rest of the classes would be the audience. The classes at the end of the hall marched to the auditorium first.

There were classes on both sides of the hall near my

room, and the space for the marchers was narrow. Some of the children had large cardboard cartons over them and were supposed to be packages of cigarettes or sports cars. These costumes had trouble getting through. Then there was Jennifer. She was last in line. She looked neither to the right nor to the left but slightly up toward the ceiling. I kept my eye on her hoping she'd say "Hi" so that I wouldn't feel so alone standing there. She didn't. Instead, well, I almost didn't believe what I actually saw her do.

But before I tell what I saw her do, I have to tell about Cynthia. Every grown-up in the whole U.S. of A. thinks that Cynthia is perfect. She is pretty and neat and smart. I guess that makes perfect to almost any grown-up. Since she lives in the same apartment house as we do, and since my mother is a grown-up, and since my mother thinks that she is perfect, my mother had tried hard to have us become friends since we first moved to town. My mother would drop hints. HINT: Why don't you call Cynthia and ask her if she would like to show you where the library is? Then you can both eat lunch here. Or HINT: Why don't you run over and play with Cynthia while I unpack the groceries?

It didn't take me long to discover that what Cynthia was, was not perfect. The word for what Cynthia was, was *mean*.

Here's an example of mean. There was a little boy in our building who had moved in about a month before we did. His name was Johann; that's German for John. He moved from Germany and didn't speak English yet. He loved Cynthia. Because she was so pretty, I guess. He followed her around and said, "Cynsssia, Cynsssia." Cynthia always made fun of him. She would stick her tongue between her teeth and say, "Th,

th, th, th, th. My name is Cyn-*th*-ia not Cyn-*sss*-ia." Johann
would smile and say, "Cyn-*sss*-ia." Cynthia would stick out
her tongue and say, "Th, th, th, th, th." And then she'd walk
away from him. I liked Johann. I wished he would follow me
around. I would have taught him English, and I would never
even have minded if he called me Elizabessss. Another word
for what Cynthia was, was *two-faced*. Because every time some
grown-up was around, she was sweet to Johann. She'd smile at
him and pat his head . . . only until the grown-up left.

And another thing: Cynthia certainly didn't need me for
a friend. She had a very good friend called Dolores who also
lived in the apartment house. They told secrets and giggled
together whenever I got into the elevator with them. So I got
into the habit of leaving for school before they did. Sometimes, on weekends, they'd be in the elevator when I got on;
I'd act as if they weren't there. I had to get off the elevator
before they did because I lived on the second floor, and they
lived on the sixth. Before I'd get off the elevator, I'd take my
fists, and fast and furious, I'd push every floor button just the
second before I got out. I'd step out of the elevator and watch
the dial stopping at every floor on the way up. Then I'd skip
home to our apartment.

For Halloween Cynthia wore everything real ballerinas
wear: leotards and tights and ballet slippers and a tutu. A tutu
is a little short skirt that ballerinas wear somewhere around
their waists. Hers looked like a nylon net doughnut floating
around her middle. Besides all the equipment I listed above,
Cynthia wore rouge and eye make-up and lipstick and a tiara.
She looked glamorous, but I could tell that she felt plenty

chilly in that costume. Her teeth were chattering. She wouldn't put on a sweater.

As we were standing in the hall waiting for our turn to go to the auditorium, and as Jennifer's class passed, Cynthia was turned around talking to Dolores. Dolores was dressed as a Pilgrim. They were both whispering and giggling. Probably about Jennifer.

Here's what Jennifer did. As she passed Cynthia, she reached out and quicker than a blink unsnapped the tutu. I happened to be watching her closely, but even I didn't believe that she had really done it. Jennifer clop-clopped along in the line with her eyes still up toward the ceiling and passed me a note almost without my knowing. She did it so fast that I wasn't even sure she did it until I felt the note in my hand and crunched it beneath my apron to hide it. Jennifer never took her eyes off the ceiling or broke out of line for even half a step.

I wanted to make sure that everyone saw Cynthia with her tutu down, so I pointed my finger at her and said, "O-o-o-o-oh!" I said it loud. Of course, that made everyone on both sides of the aisle notice her and start to giggle.

Cynthia didn't have sense enough to be embarrassed. She loved attention so much that she didn't care if her tutu had fallen. She stepped out of it, picked it up, shook it out, floated it over her head, and anchored it back around her waist. She touched her hands to her hair, giving it little pushes the way women do who have just come out of the beauty parlor. I hoped she was itchy.

Finally, our class got to the auditorium. After I sat down,

I opened the note, holding both my hands under my Pilgrim apron. I slowly slipped my hands out and glanced at the note. I was amazed at what I saw. Jennifer's note looked like this:

Meet for Trick or Treat
at
Half after six P.M. o'clock
of this evening.
By the same tree.
Bring two (2) bags.
Those were good cookies

I studied the note a long time. I thought about the note as I watched the Halloween parade; I wondered if Jennifer used a quill pen. You can guess that I didn't win any prizes for my costume. Neither did Cynthia. Neither did Jennifer (even though I thought she should have). We all marched across the stage wearing our masks and stopped for a curtsy or bow (depending on whether you were a girl or a boy) in front of the judges who were sitting at a table in the middle of the stage. Some of the girls who were disguised as boys forgot themselves and curtsied. Then we marched off. Our class was still seated when Jennifer clop-clopped across the stage in those crazy Pilgrim slippers. She didn't wear a mask at all. She wore a big brown paper bag over her head and *there were no holes cut out for her eyes.* Yet, she walked up the stairs, across the stage, stopped and curtsied, and walked off without tripping or falling or walking out of those gigantic shoes.

Our family rushed through supper that night. But the trick or treaters started coming even before we finished. Most of the early ones were bitsy kids who had to bring their mothers to reach the door bells for them.

I didn't tell my parents about Jennifer. I mentioned to my mother that I was meeting a friend at 6:30, and we were going to trick or treat together. Mom just asked, "Someone from school?" and I just said, "Yes."

The days start getting short, and the evenings start getting cool in late October. So I had to wear my old ski jacket over my costume. I looked like a Pilgrim who had made a bad trade with the Indians. Jennifer was waiting. She was leaning against the tree. She had put on stockings. They were long black cotton stockings, and she wore a huge black shawl. She smelled a little bit like moth balls, but I happen to especially like that smell in autumn.

"Hi," I said.

"I'll take the bigger bag," she replied.

She didn't say "please."

I held out the bags. She took the bigger one. She didn't say "thank you." Her manners were unusual. I guessed that witches never said "please" and never said "thank you." All my life my mother had taught me a politeness vocabulary. I didn't mind. I thought that "please" and "thank you" made conversation prettier, just as bows and lace make dresses prettier. I was full of admiration for how easily Jennifer managed without bows or lace or "please" or "thank you."

She opened her bag, stuck her head way down inside, and said:

> *"Bag, sack, parcel post,*
> *Fill thyself*
> *With goodies most."*

She lifted her head out of the bag and tightened her shawl. "We can go now," she said.

"Don't you mean 'Bag, sack, parcel, *poke*'?" I asked. "Parcel *post* is the mail; *poke* is a name for a bag."

Jennifer was walking with her head up, eyes up. She shrugged her shoulders and said, "Poetic license. *Poke* doesn't rhyme."

I shrugged my shoulders and started walking with her. Jennifer disappeared behind a tree. No master spirit had taken her away. She reappeared in a minute, pulling a wagon. It was the usual kind of child's wagon, but to make the sides taller, she had stretched a piece of chicken wire all along the inner rim. Jennifer pulled the wagon, carried her bag, clutched her shawl, and clop-clopped toward the first house. I walked.

I had been trick or treating for a number of years. I began as a bitsy kid, and my mother rang the door bells for me, as other mothers were ringing them for those other bitsy kids that night. I had been a nurse, a mouse (I had worn my sleepers with the feet in), and other things. I had been a Pilgrim before, too. I mentioned that I had been a Pilgrim the year before. All I mean to say is that I'd been trick or treating for years and years and years, and I'd seen lots of trick or treaters come to our house, but I'd never, never, never seen a performance like Jennifer's.

This is the way Jennifer operated: 1. She left the wagon outside the door of the house and out of sight of her victim. 2. She rang the bell. 3. Instead of smiling and saying "trick or treat," she said nothing when the people came to the door. 4. She half fell against the door post and said, "I would like just a drink of water." 5. She breathed hard. 6. The lady or man who answered would say, "Of course," and would bring her a drink of water. 7. As she reached out to get the water, she dropped her big, empty bag. 8. The lady or man noticed how empty it was and said, "Don't you want just a little something?" 9. The lady or man poured stuff into Jennifer's bag. 10. The lady or man put a little something in my bag, too. 11. Jennifer and I left the house. 12. Jennifer dumped the treats into the wagon. 13. Jennifer clop-clopped to the next house with the bag empty again. 14. I walked.

Jennifer did this at every house. She always drank a glass of water. She always managed to drop her empty bag. I asked her how she could drink so much water. She must have had about twenty-four glasses. She didn't answer. She shrugged her shoulders and walked with her head up, eyes up. I sort of remembered something about a water test for witches. But I also sort of remembered that it was something about witches being able to float on water that was outside their bodies, not water that was inside their bodies.

I asked Jennifer why she didn't wear a mask. She answered that one disguise was enough. She told me that all year long she was a witch, disguised as a perfectly normal girl; on Halloween she became undisguised. She may be a witch, I thought, and, of course, she was a girl. But perfect never! And normal never!

I can say that Jennifer collected more treats on that Halloween than I had in all my years put together including the time I was a mouse in my sleepers with the feet in. Because I was with Jennifer each time she went into her act, I managed to collect more treats on that Halloween than I ever had before but not nearly as many as Jennifer. My bag was heavy, though.

Jennifer and I parted about a block from my apartment house. My bag was so heavy that I could hardly hold it with one hand as I pushed the button for the elevator. I put the bag on the floor while I waited. When the elevator arrived, I leaned over to pick up my bundle and heard my Pilgrim dress go *r-r-r-r-r-i-p*. I arrived at our apartment tired and torn, but happy. Happy because I had had a successful Halloween; happy because I had not met Cynthia on the elevator; and happy because my costume had ripped. I wouldn't have to be an itchy Pilgrim another Halloween.

(Note: "A Halloween to Remember" is taken from Chapters 1 and 2 of *Jennifer, Hecate, Macbeth, William McKinley, and Me, Elizabeth.*)

Eleanor Estes

THE GHOST
IN THE ATTIC

JANE CAME SKIPPING up the street. What a good day it had been so far! And it was going to be even better, of that she was sure. It had been a good day in school because the drawing teacher, Miss Partridge, who visited every class in town once in the fall, once in the winter, and once in the spring, had paid her autumn visit that day.

Everyone in Jane's class had drawn an autumn leaf. Everyone in Rufus' a pumpkin. Everyone in Joe's an apple. All the children in the grammar schools came home with a drawing fluttering in the wind—a drawing of a pumpkin, an apple, or an autumn leaf. It is true that sometimes the children grew tired of drawing leaves, pumpkins, and apples.

However, Miss Partridge never thought of letting them draw anything else.

Still, no matter what they had to draw, the children loved the day of Miss Partridge's visit: first, because all studies would be swept aside for the sake of autumn leaves and pumpkins; secondly, because Miss Partridge was so amiable. She was always smiling, always. The children called her the smiley teacher. No one had ever seen her frown or heard her speak a cross word. Not a bit like Mr. Allgood, the music master, who was so strict he set every heart pounding like a blacksmith's hammer the minute he came in the door. Why, when Mr. Allgood entered the room, the children, without being told one word, automatically sat up in their chairs so straight that their backs would ache for the rest of the day. Chet Pudge stopped putting Jane's braids in the ink-well. Edie Ellenbach stuck her chewing gum under the seat lest she be asked to sing her music slip alone. Mr. Allgood knew the minute you opened your mouth if there was anything in it. Even Peter Frost would toe the mark and stop making slingshot bullets out of his arithmetic paper. Certainly Mr. Allgood, whom all the children called Mr. Allbad (only out of school, way in the distance), was a figure to be reckoned with.

And if it came to a toss-up, who would you rather have visit the class, Mr. Allgood or Miss Partridge? Why, Miss Partridge easily walked away with all the votes. She always said "Good! Good!" to you about your drawing, whereas your singing seemed to put Mr. Allgood in a fearful temper.

Well, so that was the kind of day it had been. A visit from the smiley teacher! There had been no sitting up straight as ramrods for her. More sticks of gum than ever were stuck in the children's mouths and oh! what a bad day it had been for Janey's braids! To cap the climax, as soon as the drawing lesson was over and the best autumn leaf drawings had been placed around the room on exhibition, Miss Partridge had produced thirty-eight orange lollipops, one for everyone in the class, and said that now they would play games, have stories, and go home fifteen minutes early.

Why all these good things in one day?

Because today was Halloween!

Jane shivered as she thought of the stories Miss Partridge had told with the shades lowered. One about a golden arm; one dreadful one about stairs and something creeping up them; and one about "my grandfather, Henry Watty," that was the most scary of all. Then they'd played some good rough games and left early.

Janey scuffled through the dry crackling leaves in the gutter, holding her drawing carefully in one hand for Mama. She felt so excited about Halloween she forgot to breathe the prayer, "Dear God, please don't let anyone buy the yellow house," which the sight of the For Sale sign usually brought to her lips. She skipped through the gate, skipped as fast as she could around the house to the back door with Catherine-the-cat racing after her. She burst into the kitchen that today smelled of hot gingerbread and ran into the Grape Room where Mrs. Shoemaker was trying on a very tight white satin gown.

Mama's mouth was full of pins, but she stopped pulling the gown down over Mrs. Shoemaker's fuzzy yellow hair long enough to look admiringly at the drawing of the autumn leaf. It would be put away later with all the apples, pumpkins, and autumn leaves in the box where Mama kept these things. She nodded her head up and down when Jane said, "May I have a piece of gingerbread?"

Jane grabbed the gingerbread and ran out to join Rufus and Joe in the barn.

"Are you gettin' ready for tonight?" she asked.

"You bet," said Joe. "Sylvie said to make a ghost. We're goin' to put her in the attic an' scare Peter Frost."

"When?"

"Tonight."

Jane sucked her breath in between her teeth. Ooh! Think of a ghost in the attic!

"Are you sure Peter Frost will come?"

"Oh, sure," said Joe. "He said to me, 'Ghosts! Ha-ha! Ghosts! No such thing!' And I said to him, 'Sure, in our attic there's a ghost.' "

"What did he say to that?" asked Jane.

"He said, 'Ghost, nothin'!' "

"And what did you say then?"

"I said, 'All right, if you don't believe me, come on over to our house at eight o'clock' and we'd show him."

"Well, we better get busy," said Rufus energetically. "What do we do first?"

"First we have to carve the head. This ghost is going to have a pumpkin head." Joe went to a dark corner of the barn and fetched a beautiful pumpkin head. The three of them set to work digging out a most startling face. And as they worked, they reviewed their grudges against Peter Frost. There were plenty of them. It was high time something should be done to even the score.

"Remember that time he made Rufus fall off the hitchin' post?"

"Remember that time he told Jane to put her mouth up against the hole in the fence and he would give her a piece of candy and he gave her a mouthful of sand instead?"

"Remember how he always is pullin' Sylvie's curls every chance he gets? And hard—so it hurts."

"Remember that time he almost got Jane arrested and she had to hide in the bread-box?"

Remember? Indeed they remembered all these insults and a great many others besides. Something just had to be done to settle the account. They worked harder and faster than they'd ever worked before.

After a while Rufus said, "I know what. We can use my teeth in this head."

"Oh, fine," said Joe. "Where are they?"

Without answering, Rufus climbed to the loft. He found the secret hiding-place under the beams where he kept some of his treasures. Here was the old tin Prince Albert tobacco box where he kept his collection of teeth. Safe apparently and quite full too. He looked at them lovingly. Some of the teeth were quite small. These were Rufus' own. But most of the collection he had found under the Grape Room window. Dr. Witty, who had lived in the yellow house before the Moffats, was a dentist. Apparently every time he pulled out a tooth, he had just tossed it out of the window. The first tooth Rufus had found one day when he was digging a hole, hoping to get a peep into China. It had filled him with the most amazed delight. In excitement he had rushed in to show it to Mama, thinking she would be as interested as he was. On the contrary, she hadn't been at all pleased about it and had said, "Throw that nasty thing away." He didn't show her his finds after that, but stored them privately in his Prince Albert box.

"Well, what are you doin' up there?" called Jane.

"Comin'," said Rufus, carefully putting them back in the box. Making his way down the ladder, he poured them out between Jane and Joe.

They looked at the teeth admiringly.

"Gee, those are swell," said Jane. "Look at that one, will you?" she said, pointing to an enormous one.

"Yeh," agreed Rufus, looking at it with pride. "Old Natby the blacksmith gave me that one. He said he'd been shoein' an old mare one day and that tooth fell out of her mouth. He said it was the biggest he'd ever seen."

They stuck the teeth in the pumpkin head and at last it was finished. They looked at their work with satisfaction. Phew! She looked gruesome, particularly with that old mare's tooth hanging over her lower lip. Twilight was approaching and they had difficulty in seeing clearly. As it grew darker, they automatically lowered their voices. Now they were talking in whispers, putting the finishing touches on their plan for the night. They began to feel a creepy uneasiness. Their own ideas scared them and sent prickles up and down their spines. They jumped when Sylvie came to the kitchen door and called them to supper, and then tore from the barn as though all the hobyahs, pookas, and goblins in the world were at their heels.

The light from the kitchen spread a warm welcome to them. From up and down the street they could hear the different whistles and calls that summoned the other children in the block home to their dinners. Pookas, hobyahs, and goblins fled . . . temporarily. The five Moffats sat down around the kitchen table. As they ate, the oil lamp in the middle of the table sputtered and sent little curls of black smoke to the top of the glass chimney.

"A wind is rising," said Mama.

The children exchanged pleased glances. A wind! So much the better.

Jane whispered to Sylvie, "Have you had a chance to bring the Madame upstairs?" For Madame-the-bust was to be the ghost this night.

"Not yet," Sylvie whispered back. "There's plenty of time."

"Plenty of time!" echoed Jane impatiently. "Supposin' Peter Frost comes before everything's ready?" She couldn't eat another bite. Rufus had finished too. Finally the others put down their spoons. Dinner was over.

"Now," said Mama, "I see no reason, even if it is Halloween, why I shouldn't leave you four children. Mrs. Pudge wants me to talk over plans for her silver wedding anniversary dress, so I think I'll go tonight. Now don't be gallivanting through the streets after eight o'clock. And, Joey, please tie the garbage pail to the back porch or some of those street hoodlums will be trying to tie it to the lamp post. And see that the rake and anything else that's movable is locked in the barn. I won't be very late." Then she put on the black velvet hat with the blue violets that matched her eyes and went out.

How still and empty the house suddenly became without Mama in it! Inside not a sound except the ticking of the clock in the sitting-room and the creaking of the cane rocking-chair that no one was sitting in. Outside the wind rustled in the trees and a dog that sounded miles away howled mournfully. The children sat hushed and motionless. Suddenly a hot coal fell in the grate. Catherine-the-cat jumped from her place under the stove, arched her back, and bristled her tail. The children broke into screams of laughter and the house became friendly again.

"Well," said Sylvie, "we'd better hurry. First the pumpkin. Who'll get that?"

Who indeed? Who would go out in that dark barn and get the pumpkin head? No one answered, so Joe and Jane were sent.

"We'll stand in the door," said Sylvie.

Breathlessly, Joe and Jane tore to the barn, snatched up the fierce-looking pumpkin head, and tore back into the warm kitchen.

"Now the Madame," said Sylvie, solemnly lighting the smallest oil lamp and leading the way into the Grape Room. Catherine-the-cat leaped ahead of her, wagging her tail restlessly. What was the matter with Catherine tonight, anyway? She kept meowing and meowing and following them all around. Sylvie set the lamp carefully on the table. Catherine-the-cat sat in the shadow. Her yellow eyes shone with a knowing gleam.

"Look at Catherine," said Jane. "She's watchin' us and watchin' us."

"Let her watch," said Sylvie as she carefully removed Mrs. Shoemaker's white satin gown from Madame-the-bust. Then she grasped Madame tightly in her arms.

"You carry the pumpkin, Joe. And Rufus, you bring your scooter. Jane can carry the sheets."

Slowly the procession made its way out of the Grape Room, into the hall, up the stairs to the second floor. Joe led the way with his pocket flashlight. From the hall upstairs, a stepladder led to the attic which did not have a regular door but a hatch which Joe had to push up with his shoulders. It fell open with a groan and the strange musty smell of the attic greeted them. Joe set the head on the floor and flashed the light down the stepladder so the others could see to climb up.

Sylvie hoisted Madame up before her and climbed in. Then Rufus handed up his scooter and hoisted himself in. As Jane was making her way up, Catherine-the-cat leaped past her and disappeared into the dark recesses of the attic. Jane bit her tongue but managed to keep from screaming. That cat! She was always doing unexpected things behind you.

The four Moffats stood around the entrance, the nearest point to the kitchen, to safety. Joe's tiny flashlight scarcely penetrated the darkness of the attic. But they knew what was up here all right without seeing. Dr. Witty had had many different hobbies. Collecting and stuffing wild animals and birds was one of them. He stored these in the attic in the yellow house. In one corner was a stuffed owl. In another, a stuffed wildcat. And all around were a great many little stuffed partridges and quail. The four children shivered, partly from cold, partly from excitement.

"Oh, let's hurry and get out of this place," said Jane.

They placed the scooter in the corner by the owl. Then they put Madame on the scooter, put the pumpkin head with its ominous, gaping mouth on her headless neck, and draped the sheets about her. They tied one end of the rope to the scooter and made a loop in the other end in order to be able to pull the ghost around easily. The end of the rope with the loop they placed near the hatchway.

"All right," said Sylvie. "Now let's see how she looks."

They went to the head of the ladder. Joe flashed his light on Madame—Madame-the-bust no longer, or Mrs. Shoemaker or Miss Nippon either, but Madame-the-ghost!

"Phew!" he whistled.

"Boy, oh, boy!" said Rufus.

"Oh," shivered Jane, "come on."

As fast as they could, they pushed the hatch back in place and hurried helter-skelter to the kitchen where they warmed their hands over the kitchen fire.

"Boy, oh, boy!" said Rufus again, "what a ghost!"

Then they all put on the most fearful masks that Sylvie had made for them. And just in the nick of time too, for here was Peter Frost stamping on the back porch.

"Hey there, Moffats," he said witheringly. "Where's your old ghost then?"

Oh, his arrogance was insufferable.

"Don't worry," said Sylvie, "you'll see her all right. But you must be quiet."

"Haw-haw," jeered Peter Frost.

But he stopped short, for out of the night came a long-drawn howl, a howl of reproach.

Sylvie, Joe, Jane, and Rufus had the same thought. Catherine-the-cat! They had forgotten her up there with the ghost. But Peter Frost! Why, he knew nothing of that of course, and although he was inclined to toss the matter lightly aside, still he blanched visibly when again from some mysterious dark recess of the house came the same wild howl.

The four Moffats knew when to be silent and they were silent now. So was Peter Frost. So was the whole house. It was so silent it began to speak with a thousand voices. When Mama's rocking-chair creaked, Peter Frost looked at it as though he expected to see the ghost sitting right in it. Somewhere a shutter came unfastened and banged against the house with persistent regularity. The clock in the sitting-room ticked slowly, painfully, as though it had a lump in its throat, then stopped altogether. Even the Moffats began to feel scared, particularly Rufus. He began to think this whole business on a par with G-R-I-N-D your bones in "Jack and the Beanstalk."

Peter Frost swallowed his breath with a great gulp and said in a voice a trifle less jeering, "Well, what're we waitin' for? I want to see yer old ghost."

"Very well, then," said the four Moffats in solemn voices. "Follow us."

Again they left the warm safety of the kitchen, mounted the inky black stairs to the second floor, each one holding to the belt of the one in front. When they reached the stepladder, they paused a moment to count heads.

"Aw, you don't think I'm gonna skin out without seeing your silly old ghost, do yer?" asked Peter Frost. However, blustering though his words were, there could be no doubt that his hand, the one that held on to Joe's belt, was shaking and shaking.

"Now we go up the stepladder," said Joe in a hoarse whisper. "I'll push open the hatch."

Cautiously the five mounted the stepladder. It seemed to lead to a never-ending pit of darkness.

"Why don't you light your flash?" asked Peter Frost, doing his best to sound carefree and easy.

"And scare away the ghost, I suppose," snorted Joe. "You know, a ghost isn't comin' out where there's a light and all this many people. That is, unless there's a certain one around it happens to be interested in."

Another howl interrupted Joe's words. This sounded so close to them now that the four Moffats were afraid Peter Frost would recognize the voice of Catherine-the-cat. But he didn't. He began to shake and shake more violently than ever, making the stepladder they were standing on shiver and creak.

Joe pushed the trap door up with his shoulders. It fell open with a groan just as it had done before. They all climbed in and stood on the attic floor. Except for a pale glow from the light below, the attic was in the thickest blackness. For a moment they stood there in silence. Then suddenly Joe gave a swift flash into the corner of the attic. It fell for a second on the stuffed wildcat.

Peter Frost started but said not a word.

Then swiftly Joe flashed the light in the other corner. The stuffed owl stared at them broodingly.

But Peter Frost said nothing.

And then Joe flashed his light on Madame-the-ghost herself. There she was, lurking in the corner, her orange head gaping horribly. All the children gasped, but still Peter Frost said nothing. All of a sudden, without any warning whatsoever, Madame-the-ghost started careening madly toward them. And dragging heavy chains behind her too, from the sound.

Jane called out in a shrill voice:

"Peter Frost! Peter Frost!
E-e-e-e-e-e-e-e!"

Joe flashed his light on and off rapidly. Madame-the-ghost dashed wildly round and round the attic. The same howl rent the air! The shutters banged. Then Peter Frost let out a roar of terror. That THING was after HIM. He tore around the attic room, roaring like a bull. And the ghost, dragging its horrible chains, tore after him.

"Let me go," he bellowed. But he couldn't find the hatch. Around the attic and around the attic he stumbled, kicking over stuffed partridges and quail. Finally he tripped over the wildcat and sprawled on the floor. Joe flashed his light on them for a second and when Peter Frost saw that he was sitting on the wildcat, he let out another piercing yell and leaped to his feet. He had seen now where the hatch was and he meant to escape before that ghost could catch up with him. Again he tripped and was down once more, this time with the ghost right on top of him. She would smother him with those ghastly robes of hers.

"She's got me! She's got me!" he roared.

Frantically he shook himself free of the ghost, and in wild leaps he made again for the hatch.

But now Rufus and Jane too had stood all they could of this nerve-racking business. They both began howling with fright and screaming, "Mama, Mama!" What with Peter

Frost's yelling, Catherine-the-cat's yowling, the screams of Rufus and Jane, Sylvie herself began laughing hysterically and the place sounded like bedlam. To make matters worse, the battery of Joe's flashlight gave out, so there was no way of turning on the blessed light and showing everyone there was no real ghost.

No, the ghost was real enough to Peter Frost, and as he finally reached the hatch and clattered down the stairs he thought he could still feel its cold breath on his neck and cheeks. The four Moffats followed after him, half tumbling, half sliding, until they reached the kitchen. Peter Frost tore out the back door with a bang and left the four of them there in the kitchen, breathless and sobbing and laughing all at once.

"Phew," gasped Joe. "Some ghost, I'll say!"

"'Twas real then?" said Rufus, getting ready to howl again.

"Of course not, silly," said Joe, whose courage had returned. "Come on, though. We've got to get the things down. Mama'll be home in a minute. Sylvie better carry the little lamp."

Rufus and Jane did not want to go back into that attic. They'd had enough of ghosts and goblins. But neither did they want to stay down in the kitchen alone. So up to the attic the four went once more. And with all the light made from the little lamp Rufus could see there wasn't any real ghost at all. Just Madame and the pumpkin head he'd stuck his own teeth into and his own scooter that Catherine-the-cat, caught in the loop of the rope, was dragging around and around.

Swiftly Sylvie unloosened the cat. She gave them all a

triumphant leer and leaped down the hatch with short me-ows. Next they dismantled the ghost and returned Madame to the Grape Room where Sylvie dressed her again in Mrs. Shoe-maker's new dress. The pumpkin head had received many bad cracks, but they put it in the sitting-room window with a candle lighted inside of it, where it looked quite jolly and altogether harmless.

Then they sat down to talk the evening over. They agreed the ghost had been a success.

"That'll teach him to be always tormentin' the life outta us," said Jane with a yawn.

"Sh-h-h," warned Sylvie. "Here comes Mama."

Mama came in the door. She took off her hat and wiped the tears that the wind had put there from her eyes.

"Goodness," she said. "The witches certainly must be out tonight all right enough. I just passed Peter Frost racing like sixty up the street. He muttered some gibberish about a ghost being after him. And look at Catherine! She looks as though she's preparing for a wild night. And why, for good-ness' sakes! Will you look here, please?" Mama's voice went on from the Grape Room where she had gone to hang her hat. "Just look here! Mrs. Shoemaker's dress is turned completely around. The hobgoblins must have done it." (Here Rufus smothered his laughter in his brown chubby fist.) "Well, well . . ." she continued, "let's bob for apples. . . ."

(Note: "The Ghost in the Attic" is taken from Chapter 5 of *The Moffats*.)

Madeleine L'Engle

POOR LITTLE
SATURDAY

THE WITCH WOMAN lived in a deserted, boarded-up plantation house, and nobody knew about her but me. Nobody in the nosy little town in south Georgia where I lived when I was a boy knew that if you walked down the dusty main street to where the post office ended it and then turned left and followed that road a piece until you got to the rusty iron gates of the drive to the plantation house, you could find goings-on would make your eyes pop out. It was just luck that I found out. Or maybe it wasn't luck at all. Maybe the witch woman wanted me to find out because of Alexandra. But now I wish I hadn't, because the witch woman and Alexandra are gone forever and it's much worse than if I'd never known them.

Nobody'd lived in the plantation house since the Civil War when Colonel Londermaine was killed and Alexandra Londermaine, his beautiful young wife, hung herself on the chandelier in the ballroom. A while before I was born some northerners bought it, but after a few years they stopped coming and people said it was because the house was haunted. Every few years a gang of boys or men would set out to explore the house but nobody ever found anything, and it was so well boarded up it was hard to force an entrance, so by and by the town lost interest in it. No one climbed the wall and wandered around the grounds except me.

I used to go there often during the summer because I had bad spells of malaria when sometimes I couldn't bear to lie on the iron bedstead in my room with the flies buzzing around my face, or out on the hammock on the porch with the screams and laughter of the other kids as they played, torturing my ears. My aching head made it impossible for me to read, and I would drag myself down the road, scuffling my bare, sun-burned toes in the dust, wearing the tattered straw hat that was supposed to protect me from the heat of the sun, shivering and sweating by turns. Sometimes it would seem hours before I got to the iron gates near which the brick wall was lowest. Often I would have to lie panting on the tall, prickly grass for minutes until I gathered strength to scale the wall and drop down on the other side.

But once inside the grounds it seemed cooler. One funny thing about my chills was that I didn't seem to shiver nearly as much when I could keep cool as I did at home where even the walls and the floors, if you touched them, were hot. The grounds were filled with live oaks that had grown up unchecked everywhere and afforded an almost continuous green shade. The ground was covered with ferns that were soft and cool to lie on, and when I flung myself down on my back and looked up, the roof of leaves was so thick that sometimes I couldn't see the sky at all. The sun that managed to filter through lost its bright, pitiless glare and came in soft yellow shafts that didn't burn you when they touched you.

One afternoon, a scorcher early in September, which is usually our hottest month (and by then you're fagged out by the heat, anyhow), I set out for the plantation. The heat lay coiled and shimmering on the road. When you looked at anything through it, it was like looking through a defective pane of glass. The dirt road was so hot that it burned even through my calloused feet, and as I walked clouds of dust rose in front of me and mixed with the shimmying of the heat. I thought I'd never make the plantation. Sweat was running into my eyes, but it was cold sweat, and I was shivering so that my teeth chattered as I walked. When I managed finally to fling myself down on my soft green bed of ferns inside the grounds, I was seized with one of the worst chills I'd ever had in spite of the fact that my mother had given me an extra dose of quinine that morning and some 666 Malaria Medicine to boot. I shut my eyes tight and clutched the ferns with my hands and teeth to wait until the chill had passed, when I heard a soft voice call:

"Boy."

I thought at first I was delirious, because sometimes I got light-headed when my bad attacks came on; only then I remembered that when I was delirious I didn't know it; all the strange things I saw and heard seemed perfectly natural. So when the voice said, "Boy," again, as soft and clear as the mockingbird at sunrise, I opened my eyes.

Kneeling near me on the ferns was a girl. She must have been about a year younger than I. I was almost sixteen so I guess she was fourteen or fifteen. She was dressed in a blue and white gingham dress; her face was very pale, but the kind of paleness that's supposed to be, not the sickly pale kind that was like mine showing even under the tan. Her eyes were big and very blue. Her hair was dark brown and she wore it parted in the middle in two heavy braids that were swinging in front of her shoulders as she peered into my face.

"You don't feel well, do you?" she asked. There was no trace of concern or worry in her voice. Just scientific interest.

I shook my head. "No," I whispered, almost afraid that if I talked she would vanish, because I had never seen anyone here before, and I thought that maybe I was dying because I felt so awful, and I thought maybe that gave me the power to see the ghost. But the girl in blue and white checked gingham seemed as I watched her to be good flesh and blood.

"You'd better come with me," she said. "She'll make you all right."

"Who's she?"

"Oh—just Her," she said.

My chill had begun to recede by then, so when she got up off her knees, I scrambled up, too. When she stood up her dress showed a white ruffled petticoat underneath it, and bits of green moss had left patterns on her knees and I didn't think that would happen to the knees of a ghost, so I followed her as she led the way toward the house. She did not go up the sagging, half-rotted steps that led to the veranda, about whose white pillars wisteria vines climbed in wild profusion, but went around to the side of the house where there were slanting doors to a cellar. The sun and rain had long since blistered and washed off the paint, but the doors looked clean and were free of the bits of bark from the eucalyptus tree that leaned nearby and that had dropped its bits of dusty peel on either side; so I knew that these cellar stairs must frequently be used.

The girl opened the cellar doors. "You go down first," she said. I went down the cellar steps, which were stone and cool against my bare feet. As she followed me she closed the cellar doors after her and as I reached the bottom of the stairs we were in pitch darkness. I began to be very frightened until her soft voice came out of the black.

"Boy, where are you?"

"Right here."

"You'd better take my hand. You might stumble."

We reached out and found each other's hands in the darkness. Her fingers were long and cool and they closed firmly around mine. She moved with authority as though she knew her way with the familiarity born of custom.

"Poor Sat's all in the dark," she said, "but he likes it that way. He likes to sleep for weeks at a time. Sometimes he snores awfully. Sat, darling!" she called gently. A soft, bubbly, blowing sound came in answer, and she laughed happily. "Oh, Sat, you are sweet!" she said, and the bubbly sound came again. Then the girl pulled at my hand and we came out into a huge and dusty kitchen. Iron skillets, pots, and pans were still hanging on either side of the huge stove, and there was a rolling pin and a bowl of flour on the marble-topped table in the middle of the room. The girl took a lighted candle off the shelf.

"I'm going to make cookies," she said as she saw me looking at the flour and the rolling pin. She slipped her hand out of mine. "Come along." She began to walk more rapidly. We left the kitchen, crossed the hall, went through the dining room, its old mahogany table thick with dust, although sheets covered the pictures on the walls. Then we went into the ballroom. The mirrors lining the walls were spotted and discolored; against one wall was a single delicate gold chair, its seat cushioned with pale rose and silver woven silk; it seemed extraordinarily well preserved. From the ceiling hung the huge chandelier from which Alexandra Londermaine had hung herself, its prisms catching and breaking up into a hundred colors the flickering of the candle and the few shafts of light that managed to slide in through the boarded-up windows. As we crossed the ballroom, the girl began to dance by herself, gracefully, lightly, so that her full, blue and white checked gingham skirts flew out around her. She looked at herself with pleasure in the old mirrors as she danced, the candle flaring and guttering in her right hand.

"You've stopped shaking. Now what will I tell Her?" she said as we started to climb the broad mahogany staircase. It was very dark so she took my hand again, and before we had reached the top of the stairs I obliged her by being seized by another chill. She felt my trembling fingers with satisfaction. "Oh, you've started again. That's good." She slid open one of the huge double doors at the head of the stairs.

·   ·   ·

As I looked in to what once must have been Colonel
Londermaine's study, I thought that surely what I saw was a
scene in a dream or a vision in delirium. Seated at the huge
table in the center of the room was the most extraordinary
woman I had ever seen. I felt that she must be very beautiful,
although she would never have fulfilled any of the standards
of beauty set by our town. Even though she was seated, I felt
that she must be immensely tall. Piled up on the table in front
of her were several huge volumes, and her finger was marking
the place in the open one in front of her, but she was not
reading. She was leaning back in the carved chair, her head
resting against a piece of blue and gold embroidered silk that
was flung across the chair back, one hand gently stroking a
fawn that lay sleeping in her lap. Her eyes were closed and
somehow I couldn't imagine what color they would be. It
wouldn't have surprised me if they had been shining amber or
the deep purple of her velvet robe. She had a great quantity of
hair, the color of mahogany in firelight, which was cut quite
short and seemed to be blown wildly about her head like
flame. Under her closed eyes were deep shadows, and lines of
pain were about her mouth. Otherwise there were no marks of
age on her face but I would not have been surprised to learn
that she was any age in the world—a hundred or twenty-five.
Her mouth was large and mobile, and she was singing something in a deep, rich voice. Two cats, one black, one white,
were coiled up, each on a book, and as we opened the doors a
leopard stood up quietly beside her but did not snarl or move.
It simply stood there and waited, watching us.

The girl nudged me and held her finger to her lips to
warn me to be quiet, but I would not have spoken—could not,

anyhow, my teeth were chattering so from my chill, which I had completely forgotten, so fascinated was I by this woman sitting back with her head against the embroidered silk, soft, deep sounds coming out of her throat. At last these sounds resolved themselves into words, and we listened to her as she sang. The cats slept indifferently, but the leopard listened, too:

> I sit high in my ivory tower,
>   The heavy curtains drawn.
> I've many a strange and lustrous flower,
>   A leopard and a fawn
>
> Together sleeping by my chair
>   And strange birds softly winging,
> And ever pleasant to my ear
>   Twelve maidens' voices singing.
>
> Here is my magic maps' array,
>   My mystic circle's flame.
> With symbol's art He lets me play,
>   The unknown my domain,
>
> And as I sit here in my dream
>   I see myself awake,
> Hearing a torn and bloody scream,
>   Feeling my castle shake . . .

Her song wasn't finished but she opened her eyes and looked at us. Now that his mistress knew we were here, the leopard seemed ready to spring and devour me at one gulp, but she put her hand on his sapphire-studded collar to restrain him.

"Well, Alexandra," she said, "whom have we here?"

The girl, who still held my hand in her long, cool fingers, answered, "It's a boy."

"So I see. Where did you find him?"

The voice sent shivers up and down my spine.

"In the fern bed. He was shaking. See? He's shaking now. Is he having a fit?" Alexandra's voice was filled with pleased interest.

"Come here, boy," the woman said.

As I didn't move, Alexandra gave me a push, and I advanced slowly. As I came near, the woman pulled one of the leopard's ears gently, saying, "Lie down, Thammuz." The beast obeyed, flinging itself at her feet. She held her hand out to me as I approached the table. If Alexandra's fingers felt firm and cool, hers had the strength of the ocean and the coolness of jade. She looked at me for a long time and I saw that her eyes were deep blue, much bluer than Alexandra's, so dark as to be almost black. When she spoke again her voice was warm and tender: "You're burning up with fever. One of the malaria bugs?" I nodded. "Well, we'll fix that for you."

When she stood and put the sleeping fawn down by the leopard, she was not as tall as I had expected her to be; nevertheless she gave an impression of great height. Several of the bookshelves in one corner were emptied of books and filled with various shaped bottles and retorts. Nearby was a large skeleton. There was an acid-stained washbasin, too; that whole section of the room looked like part of a chemist's or physicist's laboratory. She selected from among the bottles a small, amber-colored one and poured a drop of the liquid it contained into a glass of water. As the drop hit the water, there was a loud hiss and clouds of dense smoke arose. When they had drifted away, she handed the glass to me and said, "Drink. Drink, my boy!"

My hand was trembling so that I could scarcely hold the glass. Seeing this, she took it from me and held it to my lips.

"What is it?" I asked.

"Drink it," she said, pressing the rim of the glass against my teeth. On the first swallow I started to choke and would have pushed the stuff away, but she forced the rest of the burning liquid down my throat. My whole body felt on fire. I felt flame flickering in every vein, and the room and everything in it swirled around. When I had regained my equilibrium to a certain extent, I managed to gasp out again, "What is it?"

She smiled and answered,

> "Nine peacocks' hearts, four bats' tongues,
> A pinch of moon dust, and a hummingbird's lungs."

Then I asked a question I would never have dared ask if it hadn't been that I was still half drunk from the potion I had swallowed. "Are you a witch?"

She smiled again and answered, "I make it my profession."

Since she hadn't struck me down with a flash of lightning, I went on. "Do you ride a broomstick?"

This time she laughed. "I can when I like."

"Is it—is it very hard?"

"Rather like a bucking bronco at first, but I've always been a good horsewoman, and now I can manage very nicely. I've finally progressed to sidesaddle, though I still feel safer astride. I always rode my horse astride. Still, the best witches ride sidesaddle, so . . . Now run along home. Alexandra has lessons to study and I must work. Can you hold your tongue or must I make you forget?"

"I can hold my tongue."

She looked at me and her eyes burnt into me like the potion she had given me to drink. "Yes, I think you can," she said. "Come back tomorrow if you like. Thammuz will show you out."

The leopard rose and led the way to the door. As I hesitated, unwilling to tear myself away, it came back and pulled gently but firmly on my trouser leg.

"Good-bye, boy," the witch woman said. "And you won't have any more chills and fever."

"Good-bye," I answered. I didn't say thank you. I didn't say good-bye to Alexandra. I followed the leopard out.

She let me come every day. I think she must have been lonely. After all, I was the only thing there with a life apart from hers. And in the long run the only reason I have had a life of my own is because of her. I am as much a creation of the witch woman's as Thammuz the leopard was, or the two cats, Ashtaroth and Orus. (It wasn't until many years after the last day I saw the witch woman that I learned that those were the names of the fallen angels.)

She did cure my malaria, too. My parents and the towns-people thought that I had outgrown it. I grew angry when they talked about it so lightly and wanted to tell them that it was the witch woman, but I knew that if ever I breathed a word about her I would be eternally damned. Mama thought we should write a testimonial letter to the 666 Malaria Medicine people, and maybe they'd send us a couple of dollars.

Alexandra and I became very good friends. She was a strange, aloof creature. She liked me to watch her while she danced alone in the ballroom or played on an imaginary harp —though sometimes I fancied I could hear the music. One day she took me into the drawing room and uncovered a portrait that was hung between two of the long, boarded-up windows. Then she stepped back and held her candle high so as to throw the best light on the picture. It might have been a picture of Alexandra herself, or Alexandra as she might be in five years.

"That's my mother," she said. "Alexandra Londermaine."

As far as I knew from the tales that went about town, Alexandra Londermaine had given birth to only one child, and that stillborn, before she had hung herself on the chandelier in the ballroom—and anyhow, any child of hers would have been this Alexandra's mother or grandmother. But I didn't say anything, because when Alexandra got angry she became ferocious like one of the cats and was given to leaping on me, scratching and biting. I looked at the portrait long and silently.

"You see, she has on a ring like mine," Alexandra said, holding out her left hand, on the fourth finger of which was the most beautiful sapphire and diamond ring I had ever seen —or rather, that I could ever have imagined, for it was a ring apart from any owned by even the most wealthy of the townsfolk. Then I realized that Alexandra had brought me in here and unveiled the portrait simply that she might show me the ring to better advantage, for she had never worn a ring before.

"Where did you get it?"

"Oh, She got it for me last night."

"Alexandra," I asked suddenly, "how long have you been here?"

"Oh, awhile."

"But how long?"

"Oh, I don't remember."

"But you must remember."

"I don't. I just came—like Poor Sat."

"Who's Poor Sat?" I asked, thinking for the first time of whoever it was that had made the gentle bubbly noises at Alexandra the day she found me in the fern bed.

"Why, we've never shown you Sat, have we!" she exclaimed. "I'm sure it's all right, but we'd better ask Her first."

So we went to the witch woman's room and knocked. Thammuz pulled the door open with his strong teeth and the witch woman looked up from some sort of experiment she was making with test tubes and retorts. The fawn, as usual, lay sleeping near her feet. "Well?" she said.

"Is it all right if I take him to see Poor Little Saturday?" Alexandra asked her.

"Yes, I suppose so," she answered. "But no teasing." And she turned her back to us and bent again over her test tubes as Thammuz nosed us out of the room.

We went down to the cellar. Alexandra lit a lamp and took me back to the corner farthest from the doors, where there was a stall. In the stall was a two-humped camel. I couldn't help laughing as I looked at him because he grinned at Alexandra so foolishly, displaying all his huge buckteeth and blowing bubbles through them.

"She said we weren't to tease him," Alexandra said severely, rubbing her cheek against the preposterous splotchy hair that seemed to be coming out, leaving bald pink spots of skin on his long nose.

"But what—" I started.

"She rides him sometimes." Alexandra held out her hand while he nuzzled against it, scratching his rubbery lips against the diamond and sapphire of her ring. "Mostly She talks to him. She says he is very wise. He goes up to Her room sometimes and they talk and talk. I can't understand a word they say. She says it's Hindustani and Arabic. Sometimes I can remember little bits of it, like: *iderow, sorcabatcha,* and *anna bibed bech.* She says I can learn to speak with them when I finish learning French and Greek."

Poor Little Saturday was rolling his eyes in delight as Alexandra scratched behind his ears. "Why is he called Poor Little Saturday?" I asked.

Alexandra spoke with a ring of pride in her voice. "I named him. She let me."

"But why did you name him that?"

"Because he came last winter on the Saturday that was the shortest day of the year, and it rained all day so it got light later and dark earlier than it would have if it had been nice, so it really didn't have as much of itself as it should, and I felt so sorry for it I thought maybe it would feel better if we named him after it. . . . She thought it was a nice name!" She turned on me suddenly.

"Oh, it is! It's a fine name!" I said quickly, smiling to myself as I realized how much greater was this compassion of Alexandra's for a day than any she might have for a human being. "How did She get him?" I asked.

"Oh, he just came."

"What do you mean?"

"She wanted him so he came. From the desert."

"He *walked*!"

"Yes. And swam part of the way. She met him at the beach and flew him here on the broomstick. You should have seen him. He was still all wet and looked so funny. She gave him hot coffee with things in it."

"What things?"

"Oh, just things."

Then the witch woman's voice came from behind us. "Well, children?"

It was the first time I had seen her out of her room. Thammuz was at her right heel, the fawn at her left. The cats, Ashtaroth and Orus, had evidently stayed upstairs. "Would you like to ride Saturday?" she asked me.

Speechless, I nodded. She put her hand against the wall and a portion of it slid down into the earth so that Poor Little Saturday was free to go out. "She's sweet, isn't she?" the witch woman asked me, looking affectionately at the strange, bumpy-kneed, splay-footed creature. "Her grandmother was very good to me in Egypt once. Besides, I love camel's milk."

"But Alexandra said she was a he!" I exclaimed.

"Alexandra's the kind of woman to whom all animals are he except cats, and all cats are she. As a matter of fact,

Ashtaroth and Orus are she, but it wouldn't make any difference to Alexandra if they weren't. Go on out, Saturday. Come on!"

Saturday backed out, bumping her bulging knees and ankles against her stall, and stood under a live oak tree. "Down," the witch woman said. Saturday leered at me and didn't move. "Down, *sorcabatcha!*" the witch woman commanded, and Saturday obediently got down on her knees. I clambered up onto her, and before I had managed to get at all settled she rose with such a jerky motion that I knocked my chin against her front hump and nearly bit my tongue off. Round and round Saturday danced while I clung wildly to her front hump and the witch woman and Alexandra rolled on the ground with laughter. I felt as though I were on a very unseaworthy vessel on the high seas, and it wasn't long before I felt violently seasick as Saturday pranced among the live oak trees, sneezing delicately.

At last the witch woman called out, "Enough!" and Saturday stopped in her traces, nearly throwing me, and knelt laboriously. "It was mean to tease you," the witch woman said, pulling my nose gently. "You may come sit in my room with me for a while if you like."

There was nothing I liked better than to sit in the witch woman's room and to watch her while she studied from her books, worked out strange-looking mathematical problems, argued with the zodiac, or conducted complicated experiments with her test tubes and retorts, sometimes filling the room with sulphurous odors or flooding it with red or blue light. Only once was I afraid of her, and that was when she danced with the skeleton in the corner. She had the room flooded with a strange red glow, and I almost thought I could see the flesh covering the bones of the skeleton as they danced together like lovers. I think she had forgotten that I was sitting there, half hidden in the wing chair, because when they had finished dancing and the skeleton stood in the corner again, his bones shining and polished, devoid of any living trappings, she stood with her forehead against one of the deep red velvet curtains that covered the boarded-up windows and tears streamed down her cheeks. Then she went back to her test tubes and worked feverishly. She never alluded to the incident and neither did I.

As winter drew on she let me spend more and more time in the room. Once I gathered up courage enough to ask her about herself, but I got precious little satisfaction.

"Well, then, are you maybe one of the northerners who bought the place?"

"Let's leave it at that, boy. We'll say that's who I am. Did you know that my skeleton was old Colonel Londermaine? Not so old, as a matter of fact; he was only thirty-seven when he was killed at the battle of Bunker Hill—or am I getting him confused with his great grandfather, Rudolph Londermaine? Anyhow he was only thirty-seven, and a fine figure of a man, and Alexandra only thirty when she hung herself for love of him on the chandelier in the ballroom. Did you know that the fat man with the red mustache has been trying to cheat your father? His cow will give sour milk for seven days. Run along now and talk to Alexandra. She's lonely."

When the winter had turned to spring and the camellias and azaleas and Cape Jessamine had given way to the more lush blooms of early May, I kissed Alexandra for the first time, very clumsily. The next evening when I managed to get away from the chores at home and hurried out to the plantation, she gave me her sapphire and diamond ring, which she had swung for me on a narrow bit of turquoise satin.

"It will keep us both safe," she said, "if you wear it always. And then when we're older we can get married and you can give it back to me. Only you mustn't let anyone see it, ever, ever, or She'd be very angry."

I was afraid to take the ring but when I demurred Alexandra grew furious and started kicking and biting and I had to give in.

Summer was almost over before my father discovered the ring hanging about my neck. I fought like a witch boy to keep him from pulling out the narrow ribbon and seeing the ring, and indeed the ring seemed to give me added strength, and I had grown, in any case, much stronger during the winter than I had ever been in my life. But my father was still stronger than I, and he pulled it out. He looked at it in dead silence for a moment and then the storm broke. That was the famous Londermaine ring that had disappeared the night Alexandra Londermaine hung herself. That ring was worth a fortune. Where had I got it?

No one believed me when I said I had found it in the grounds near the house—I chose the grounds because I didn't want anybody to think I had been in the house or indeed that I was able to get in. I don't know why they didn't believe me; it still seems quite logical to me that I might have found it buried among the ferns.

It had been a long, dull year, and the men of the town were all bored. They took me and forced me to swallow quantities of corn liquor until I didn't know what I was saying or doing. When they had finished with me I didn't even manage to reach home before I was violently sick and then I was in my mother's arms and she was weeping over me. It was morning before I was able to slip away to the plantation house. I ran pounding up the mahogany stairs to the witch woman's room and opened the heavy sliding doors without knocking. She stood in the center of the room in her purple robe, her arms around Alexandra, who was weeping bitterly. Overnight the room had completely changed. The skeleton of Colonel Londermaine was gone, and books filled the shelves in the corner of the room that had been her laboratory. Cobwebs were everywhere, and broken glass lay on the floor; dust was inches thick on her worktable. There was no sign of Thammuz, Ashtaroth or Orus, or the fawn, but four birds were flying about her, beating their wings against her hair.

She did not look at me or in any way acknowledge my presence. Her arm about Alexandra, she led her out of the room and to the drawing room where the portrait hung. The birds followed, flying around and around them. Alexandra had stopped weeping now. Her face was very proud and pale, and if she saw me miserably trailing behind them she gave no notice. When the witch woman stood in front of the portrait the sheet fell from it. She raised her arm; there was a great cloud of smoke; the smell of sulphur filled my nostrils, and when the smoke was gone, Alexandra was gone, too. Only the portrait was there, the fourth finger of the left hand now bearing no ring. The witch woman raised her hand again and the sheet lifted itself up and covered the portrait. Then she went, with the birds, slowly back to what had once been her room, and still I tailed after, frightened as I had never been before in my life, or have been since.

She stood without moving in the center of the room for a long time. At last she turned and spoke to me.

"Well, boy, where is the ring?"

"They have it."

"They made you drunk, didn't they?"

"Yes."

"I was afraid something like this would happen when I gave Alexandra the ring. But it doesn't matter. . . . I'm tired. . . ." She drew her hand wearily across her forehead.

"Did I—did I tell them everything?"

"You did."

"I—I didn't know."

"I know you didn't know, boy."

"Do you hate me now?"

"No, boy, I don't hate you."

"Do you have to go away?"

"Yes."

I bowed my head. "I'm so sorry. . . ."

She smiled slightly. "The sands of time . . . cities crumble and rise and will crumble again and breath dies down and blows once more. . . ."

The birds flew madly about her head, pulling at her hair, calling into her ears. Downstairs we could hear a loud pounding, and then the crack of boards being pulled away from a window.

"Go, boy," she said to me. I stood rooted, motionless,

unable to move. "Go!" she commanded, giving me a mighty push so that I stumbled out of the room. They were waiting for me by the cellar doors and caught me as I climbed out. I had to stand there and watch when they came out with her. But it wasn't the witch woman, my witch woman. It was *their* idea of a witch woman, someone thousands of years old, a disheveled old creature in rusty black, with long wisps of gray hair, a hooked nose, and four wiry black hairs springing out of the mole on her chin. Behind her flew the four birds, and suddenly they went up, up, into the sky, directly in the path of the sun until they were lost in its burning glare.

Two of the men stood holding her tightly, although she wasn't struggling but standing there, very quiet, while the others searched the house, searched it in vain. Then as a group of them went down into the cellar I remembered, and by a flicker of the old light in the witch woman's eyes I could see that she remembered, too. Poor Little Saturday had been forgotten. Out she came, prancing absurdly up the cellar steps, her rubbery lips stretched back over her gigantic teeth, her eyes bulging with terror. When she saw the witch woman, her lord and master, held captive by two dirty, insensitive men, she let out a shriek and began to kick and lunge wildly, biting, screaming with the blood-curdling, heart-rending screams that only a camel can make. One of the men fell to the ground, holding a leg in which the bone had snapped from one of Saturday's kicks. The others scattered in terror, leaving the witch woman standing on the veranda supporting herself by clinging to one of the huge wisteria vines that curled around the columns. Saturday clambered up onto the veranda and knelt while she flung herself between the two humps.

Then off they ran, Saturday still screaming, her knees knocking together, the ground shaking as she pounded along. Down from the sun plummeted the four birds and flew after them.

Up and down I danced, waving my arms, shouting wildly until Saturday and the witch woman and the birds were lost in a cloud of dust, while the man with the broken leg lay moaning on the ground beside me.

Arthur Bowie Chrisman

AH TCHA THE SLEEPER

YEARS AGO, in southern China, lived a boy, Ah Tcha by name. Ah Tcha was an orphan, but not according to rule. A most peculiar orphan was he. It is usual for orphans to be very, very poor. That is the world-wide custom. Ah Tcha, on the contrary, was quite wealthy. He owned seven farms, with seven times seven horses to draw the plow. He owned seven mills, with plenty of breezes to spin them. Furthermore, he owned seven thousand pieces of gold, and a fine white cat.

The farms of Ah Tcha were fertile, were wide. His horses were brisk in the furrow. His mills never lacked for grain, nor wanted for wind. And his gold was good sharp gold, with not so much as a trace of copper. Surely, few orphans have been better provided for than the youth named Ah Tcha. And what a busy person was this Ah Tcha. His bed was always cold when the sun arose. Early in the morning he went from field to field, from mill to mill, urging on the people who worked for him. The setting sun always found him on his feet, hastening from here to there, persuading his laborers to more gainful efforts. And the moon of midnight often discovered him pushing up and down the little teakwood balls of a counting board, or else threading cash, placing coins upon a string. Eight farms, nine farms he owned, and more stout horses. Ten mills, eleven, another white cat. It was Ah Tcha's ambition to become the richest person in the world.

They who worked for the wealthy orphan were inclined now and then to grumble. Their pay was not beggarly, but how they did toil to earn that pay which was not beggarly. It was go, and go, and go. Said the ancient woman Nu Wu, who worked with a rake in the field: "Our master drives us as if he were a fox and we were hares in the open. Round the field and round and round, hurry, always hurry." Said Hu Shu, her husband, who bound the grain into sheaves: "Not hares, but horses. We are driven like the horses of Lung Kuan, who . . ." It's a long story.

But Ah Tcha, approaching the murmurers, said, "Pray be so good as to hurry, most excellent Nu Wu, for the clouds gather blackly, with thunder." And to the scowling husband he said, "Speed your work, I beg you, honorable Hu Shu, for the grain must be under shelter before the smoke of Evening Rice ascends."

When Ah Tcha had eaten his Evening Rice, he took lantern and entered the largest of his mills. A scampering rat drew his attention to the floor. There he beheld no less than a score of rats, some gazing at him as if undecided whether to flee or continue the feast, others gnawing—and who are you, nibbling and caring not? And only a few short whisker-lengths away sat an enormous cat, sleeping the sleep of a mossy stone. The cat was black in color, black as a crow's wing dipped in pitch, upon a night of inky darkness. That describes her coat. Her face was somewhat more black. Ah Tcha had never before seen her. She was not his cat. But his or not, he thought it a trifle unreasonable of her to sleep, while the rats held high carnival. The rats romped between her paws. Still she slept. It angered Ah Tcha. The lantern rays fell on her eyes. Still she slept. Ah Tcha grew more and more provoked. He decided then and there to teach the cat that his mill was no place for sleepy heads.

Accordingly, he seized an empty grain sack and hurled it with such exact aim that the cat was sent heels over head. "There, old Crouch-by-the-hole," said Ah Tcha in a tone of wrath. "Remember your paining ear, and be more vigilant." But the cat had no sooner regained her feet than she changed into . . . Nu Wu . . . changed into Nu Wu, the old woman who worked in the fields . . . a witch. What business she had in the mill is a puzzle. However, it is undoubtedly true that mills hold grain, and grain is worth money. And that may be an explanation. Her sleepiness is no puzzle at all. No wonder she was sleepy, after working so hard in the field, the day's length through.

The anger of Nu Wu was fierce and instant. She wagged a crooked finger at Ah Tcha, screeching: "Oh, you cruel money-grubber. Because you fear the rats will eat a pennyworth of grain you must beat me with bludgeons. You make me work like a slave all day—and wish me to work all night. You beat me and disturb my slumber. Very well, since you will not let me sleep, I shall cause you to slumber eleven hours out of every dozen. . . . Close your eyes." She swept her wrinkled hand across Ah Tcha's face. Again taking the form of a cat, she bounded downstairs.

She had scarce reached the third step descending when Ah Tcha felt a compelling desire for sleep. It was as if he had taken gum of the white poppy flower, as if he had tasted honey of the gray moon blossom. Eyes half closed, he stumbled into a grain bin. His knees doubled beneath him. Down he went, curled like a dormouse. Like a dormouse he slumbered.

From that hour began a change in Ah Tcha's fortune. The spell gripped him fast. Nine-tenths of his time was spent in sleep. Unable to watch over his laborers, they worked when they pleased, which was seldom. They idled when so inclined —and that was often, and long. Furthermore, they stole in a manner most shameful. Ah Tcha's mills became empty of grain. His fields lost their fertility. His horses disappeared— strayed, so it was said. Worse yet, the unfortunate fellow was summoned to a magistrate's *yamen*, there to defend himself in a lawsuit. A neighbor declared that Ah Tcha's huge black cat had devoured many chickens. There were witnesses who swore to the deed. They were sure, one and all, that Ah Tcha's black cat was the cat at fault. Ah Tcha was sleeping too soundly to deny that the cat was his. . . . So the magistrate could do nothing less than make the cat's owner pay damages, with all costs of the lawsuit.

Thereafter, trials at court were a daily occurrence. A second neighbor said that Ah Tcha's black cat had stolen a flock of sheep. Another complained that the cat had thieved from him a herd of fattened bullocks. Worse and worse grew the charges. And no matter how absurd, Ah Tcha, sleeping in the prisoner's cage, always lost and had to pay damages. His money soon passed into other hands. His mills were taken from him. His farms went to pay for the lawsuits. Of all his wide lands, there remained only one little acre—and it was grown up in worthless bushes. Of all his goodly buildings, there was left one little hut, where the boy spent most of his time, in witch-imposed slumber.

Now, near by in the mountain of Huge Rocks Piled, lived a greatly ferocious *loong*, or, as foreigners would say, a dragon. This immense beast, from tip of forked tongue to the end of his shadow, was far longer than a barn. With the exception of length, he was much the same as any other *loong*. His head was shaped like that of a camel. His horns were deer horns. He had bulging rabbit eyes, a snake neck. Upon his many ponderous feet were tiger claws, and the feet were shaped very like sofa cushions. He had walrus whiskers, and a breath of red-and-blue flame. His voice was like the sound of a hundred brass kettles pounded. Black fish scales covered his body, black feathers grew upon his limbs. Because of his color he was sometimes called *Oo Loong*. From that it would seem that *Oo* means neither white nor pink.

The black *loong* was not regarded with any great esteem. His habit of eating a man—two men if they were little—every day made him rather unpopular. Fortunately, he prowled only at night. Those folk who went to bed decently at nine o'clock had nothing to fear. Those who rambled well along toward midnight often disappeared with a sudden and complete thoroughness.

As every one knows, cats are much given to night skulking. The witch cat, Nu Wu, was no exception. Midnight often found her miles afield. On such a midnight, when she was roving in the form of a hag, what should approach but the black dragon. Instantly the *loong* scented prey, and instantly he made for the old witch.

There followed such a chase as never was before on land or sea. Up hill and down dale, by stream and wood and fallow, the cat woman flew and the dragon coursed after. The witch soon failed of breath. She panted. She wheezed. She stumbled on a bramble and a claw slashed through her garments. Too close for comfort. The harried witch changed shape to a cat, and bounded off afresh, half a li at every leap. The *loong* increased his pace and soon was close behind, gaining. For a most peculiar fact about the *loong* is that the more he runs the easier his breath comes, and the swifter grows his speed. Hence, it is not surprising that his fiery breath was presently singeing the witch cat's back.

In a twinkling the cat altered form once more, and as an old hag scuttled across a turnip field. She was merely an ordinarily powerful witch. She possessed only the two forms—cat and hag. Nor did she have a gift of magic to baffle or cripple the hungry black *loong*. Nevertheless, the witch was not despairing. At the edge of the turnip field lay Ah Tcha's miserable patch of thick bushes. So thick were the bushes as to be almost a wall against the hag's passage. As a hag, she could have no hope of entering such a thicket. But as a cat, she could race through without hindrance. And the dragon would be sadly bothered in following. Scheming thus, the witch dashed under the bushes—a cat once more.

Ah Tcha was roused from slumber by the most outrageous noise that had ever assailed his ears. There was such a snapping of bushes, such an awful bellowed screeching that even the dead of a century must have heard. The usually sound-sleeping Ah Tcha was awakened at the outset. He soon realized how matters stood—or ran. Luckily, he had learned of the only reliable method for frightening off the dragon. He opened his door and hurled a red, a green, and a yellow firecracker in the monster's path.

In through his barely opened door the witch cat dragged her exhausted self. "I don't see why you couldn't open the door sooner," she scolded, changing into a hag. "I circled the hut three times before you had the gumption to let me in."

"I am very sorry, good mother. I was asleep." From Ah Tcha.

"Well, don't be so sleepy again," scowled the witch, "or I'll make you suffer. Get me food and drink."

"Again, honored lady, I am sorry. So poor am I that I have only water for drink. My food is the leaves and roots of bushes."

"No matter. Get what you have—and quickly."

Ah Tcha reached outside the door and stripped a handful of leaves from a bush. He plunged the leaves into a kettle of hot water and signified that the meal was prepared. Then he lay down to doze, for he had been awake fully half a dozen minutes and the desire to sleep was returning stronger every moment.

The witch soon supped and departed, without leaving so much as half a "Thank you." When Ah Tcha awoke again, his visitor was gone. The poor boy flung another handful of leaves into his kettle and drank quickly. He had good reason for haste. Several times he had fallen asleep with the cup at his lips—a most unpleasant situation, and scalding. Having taken several sips, Ah Tcha stretched him out for a resumption of his slumber. Five minutes passed . . . ten minutes . . . fifteen. . . . Still his eyes failed to close. He took a few more sips from the cup and felt more awake than ever.

"I do believe," said Ah Tcha, "that she has thanked me by bewitching my bushes. She has charmed the leaves to drive away my sleepiness."

And so she had. Whenever Ah Tcha felt tired and sleepy —and at first that was often—he had only to drink of the bewitched leaves. At once his drowsiness departed. His neighbors soon learned of the bushes that banished sleep. They came to drink of the magic brew. There grew such a demand that Ah Tcha decided to set a price on the leaves. Still the demand continued. More bushes were planted. Money came.

Throughout the province people called for "the drink of Ah Tcha." In time they shortened it by asking for "Ah Tcha's drink," then for "Tcha's drink," and finally for "Tcha."

And that is its name at present, "Tcha," or "Tay," or "Tea," as some call it. And one kind of Tea is still called "Oo Loong"—"Black Dragon."

Phyllis Reynolds Naylor

THE WITCH'S EYE

Lynn Morley and her best friend Mouse have always suspected that their neighbor Mrs. Tuggle was a witch. Now Mrs. Tuggle is dead. But when her glass eye resurfaces, the two girls are in for new dangers and terrors.

An old book called Spells and Potions *that they find could be the answer to warding off the evil powers of the eye. Or will its charms and spells only call back the spirit of the witch herself?!*

MOUSE WAS TOSSING popcorn in the air, piece by piece, trying to catch it in her mouth. "I was reading some more of *Spells and Potions* at the bookstore this morning," she said after a bit.

"What did you find out? *Tell* me!"

"Not much. But it did say that witches hate the color red, they don't like anything made of coral, and I think I have a new charm we can use."

"You do? What is it?"

"Do you have any horseshoes?"

"No. Why would we have horseshoes? We don't have any horses."

"Well, you're supposed to nail three horseshoes to your bedpost—"

"We don't even have a bedpost."

"—and then you say these words." Mouse reached over to where her jeans were lying and pulled a slip of paper from one pocket:

> *"Suns that sear and fires that roast,*
> *Nail all evil to this post.*
> *Thrice I smite with stone or rock,*
> *With this mell I thrice do knock.*
> *One for Bod,*
> *And one for Wod,*
> *And one for Lok."*

Lynn turned her head and stared. "What's that supposed to mean?"

"How do I know? You said to look for charms and I found one so I copied it down."

Lynn snatched the paper from her. "What's 'mell'?"

"I don't know."

"What's 'Bod' and 'Wod' and 'Lok'?"

"Search me."

"Oh, for Pete's sake, Mouse, how is this going to help? All you do is nail three horseshoes to your bedpost and say these words and witches can't hurt you?"

"It didn't say anything about witches. It protects you from marsh-fever."

Lynn sat up. "Oh, Mouse, you're so *stupid!*" she yelled in exasperation. "We're not in danger from marsh-fever, we're in danger from witchcraft. I'm trying like everything to keep my family safe and you safe and everybody safe, and all you can come up with is a charm for marsh-fever. You're *dumb!*"

Mouse started to bawl, and this seemed to annoy Lynn even more.

"Oh, stop it! Stupid charms and stupid tears, and I'm the one who's doing all the worrying."

Mouse jumped up and reached for her jeans. "I'm going home."

This time Lynn's voice softened. "Oh, Mouse, I'm sorry. Really! There I go again, shooting off my mouth. I'm just plain scared and I take it out on everybody. I'm really sorry."

Mouse glared at her and plunked back down. "I'd like to see *you* sit down with *Spells and Potions* for a whole afternoon and try to make sense of it. Most of those charms were for things I never even heard of. The only other one I found is the one we already know."

"Which one is that?"

"Where you take a ring of someone who has died, wrap it in silk, bury it under an oak tree for one night, dip it in vinegar, and hold it over the flame of a candle while you recite three times: 'Wind and water, earth and sky, keep me

safe from witches.' And after that you have to wear it con-
stantly, because if you take it off for even a minute the power
is gone."

"Did we try that?"

"Don't you remember? I took the ring my grandmother
gave me before she died, and we did all that, except it fell off
once when I was playing the piano and I never went through
it all again."

Lynn settled back against the headboard, thinking.
"What if we took Mrs. Tuggle's eye, wrapped it in silk, buried
it under an oak tree, dipped it in vinegar, and held it over a
flame? Do you think that would take all its power away?"

"Where's the nearest oak tree?"

"Down the street."

"So who's going to go out in all this rain to bury the eye?
And what if it washes away in the night?"

Lynn sighed and thought some more. She almost volun-
teered. Her legs ached with restlessness. A walk—even a walk
in the rain—might help. She still felt somewhat feverish.
Rain might help that too. But she said, "What if we did only
part of it? Part of it would probably be better than nothing.
We could do everything except bury it."

"Oh, Lordy, Lynn, I don't know . . ."

"We've got to show the eye we're not afraid of it. Judith's
got a silk scarf. We'll wrap it in that for a while, then we'll go
downstairs, dip it in vinegar, hold it over a flame, and say the
charm."

Mouse crept quickly under the covers, pulled them up to
her chin, and watched while Lynn took a scarf from Judith's

dresser, Mrs. Tuggle's eye from her pocket, and wrapped the blue scarf around the green glass eye.

They left it there while they took turns reading *The Midnight Fox* to each other. Then they checked the eye. Nothing had happened. The rain outside was coming down a little harder and the wind was stronger, but the eye merely winked and looked the same as it had before.

"Okay," said Lynn. "Let's dip it in vinegar."

"Lynn, we're really asking for t-trouble," Mouse said, peering over the top of the bedspread. "How do you know that when we use the eye we're not becoming a *part* of the witchcraft instead of trying to keep it away?"

"Because we're using the witchcraft protection charm, that's why. We're not calling on devils and demons, Mouse. We're trying to get the heck away from them!"

Mouse gave a deep sigh. "Okay," she said, and climbed out of bed.

Lynn started downstairs to the kitchen, Mouse behind her, the blanket wrapped around her shoulders and trailing on the stairs.

"M-maybe we should check Stevie and make sure he's okay," Mouse said. "We're going to wake him going up and down the stairs."

"Not Stevie," said Lynn. "He sleeps like a log. Once, after I'd been sick and Mom had given me dinner in bed, I was carrying a whole tray of dishes back to the kitchen and dropped it right outside his door. Stevie didn't even wake up."

But she peeped into her brother's room to make sure. The little boy was sound asleep, breathing peacefully beneath his Donald Duck night light there on the wall. Lynn went back out and closed the door.

Down in the kitchen, she poured a cup half full of vinegar.

"What do you want to happen, Lynn? The eye to dissolve or what?" Mouse asked, watching from a distance.

"I'll take whatever we can get," Lynn said. "Even if this only gives us *half* protection from witchcraft, I'll take it." She dropped the eye in the cup, and as it sank into the vinegar, it gave off a strange hissing sound, like a snake.

Lynn jumped backward. Mouse tripped over the blanket, trying to get out of the way. They clutched each other as they cowered against the wall. A foul-smelling mist seemed to rise from the cup, but slowly the hissing stopped. Outside, the rain came down harder still. Lynn could hear it gurgling down the gutters, hitting against the pane.

When Lynn's breathing returned to normal, she crept forward and peered into the cup. The eye seemed to glisten and glow in the vinegar, giving it a strange green cast.

"W-what time will your folks be home?" Marjorie asked.

"Late. The movie isn't over until eleven, and then they're going to some friends' house. Not before one, I guess."

Since nothing else seemed to be happening with the eye, the girls got out a package of chocolate grahams and some milk. At twenty after eleven, the phone rang. Lynn bolted for the hall.

It was Mr. Morley. "Lynn, we just got to the Swansons' house in all this rain, and we wondered how things are going there. No leaks in the roof, I hope."

Lynn knew that her father was not worried about leaks in the roof. He was worried about her. "I don't hear any drips," she answered.

"Good." There was a pause. "Everything okay? Stevie in bed?"

"We just checked, Dad. He's sound asleep."

"Great. Well, we left our number by the phone, sweetheart. Call us if you need to—any reason at all."

"We will."

There was another pause. "Your mother wants to be sure all the doors are locked."

"Yeah, they are, Dad." Lynn wished that her father would stop asking questions. The more he asked, the more uneasy she became.

"Well, Main Avenue was under a foot of water near Spring Street, and I just wanted to be sure the house wasn't floating away. I think that your mother and Marie are getting ready to make a pizza, so don't worry if we're not home before two."

"Okay. Have a good time."

There was something about knowing she could reach her parents, something about having the Swansons' number by the phone that made Lynn feel better when she hung up. Brave, even. She went back into the kitchen and checked the eye. It continued its greenish glow.

"Okay," she said. "Time for the chant. You hold this match, Mouse. I'll put the eye in a spoon and hold it over the flame. We'll both say the words."

She gave Mouse a long kitchen match, and after the

flame glowed brightly, then settled down to a yellow light, Lynn put the eye in a teaspoon, held it over the flame, and the girls said the words together:

> *"Wind and water, earth and sky,*
> *Keep me safe from witches."*

Nothing happened until they said the word "witches." Then suddenly the flame flared up in a burst of fire, making the spoon too hot to hold, and Lynn dropped it. The eye rolled across the kitchen floor and came to rest against one leg of the refrigerator, winking . . . winking. . . .

"Oh, Lordy!" Mouse collapsed into a chair, clutching the blanket tightly around her. But Lynn began to smile.

"You know what we're going to do next, Mouse? Boil it."

Mouse scooted away from the table, away from Lynn. "Boil the eye?"

"Boil the eye."

Lynn got a saucepan, filled it with water, and put it on the stove.

"Lynn, don't!"

Lynn just laughed. "Boil and bubble, toil and trouble—"

"*Please*, Lynn!"

Again Lynn was conscious that she didn't feel very well. Her lips seemed changed or something, the skin around her mouth tight. She turned the flame up high.

For almost three minutes, Mouse said nothing. Sat in the corner watching Lynn. When the water was bubbling hard, Lynn walked across the floor, picked up the eye, and then, holding it above the pot of boiling water, dropped it in.

Instantly there was a flash of lightning outside the window, followed immediately by a loud thunderclap.

Mouse leaped off the chair and bolted out into the hallway.

"Take it out, Lynn!" she pleaded. "Take it out!"

Lynn hesitated, but a moment later the lightning came again, and the thunder seemed almost instantaneous. Lynn grabbed a pair of kitchen tongs, thrust them into the water, pulled out the eye, and turned the fire off. When the eye had cooled, she put it back in her pocket.

"Don't do that again, Lynn. Don't do anything more with the eye," Mouse begged. Then, "You're really acting weird, Lynn. You *look* weird."

"How?" But even as she said it, Lynn realized that her voice sounded strange even to her.

"I don't know. You've got wrinkles around your mouth."

Lynn raised one finger and felt around her lips. "They're chapped, that's all."

"Let's go upstairs and wait for your folks. Okay?" Mouse started for the stairs. "Okay?"

Mouse led the way, and Lynn followed. She stopped in the bathroom, however, and when she looked in the mirror, Lynn decided that she *did* look strange. There *were* little wrinkles around her lips, the way she looked sometimes in winter, when her skin was very dry and chapped. She smeared some lotion around her mouth.

When they reached the bedroom, Mouse said, "I don't want to sleep alone, Lynn. Stay over here with me, at least till your folks get back."

Lynn agreed. She didn't particularly want to be alone on

her side of the bedroom either, not in a storm like this. She was thinking about the lightning that had struck Mrs. Tuggle's home, burning it to the ground. If lightning struck the Morley home, she told herself, she would rush downstairs with Mouse, grab Stevie, and get him outside. She rehearsed it in her mind and that made her feel better.

She lay for a long time, listening to the rain throbbing on the roof. But she didn't feel sleepy. Her legs had that jumpy, restless feeling again, wanting to walk, to run. She tossed from one side to the other.

"Boy, I can see why you and Judith don't sleep in the same bed," Mouse said after a while. "Sleeping with you is like sleeping with a windmill, Lynn."

"I've got the jumps," Lynn told her.

They were quiet for a little longer, and then Mouse asked, "If the eye had its way, Lynn, what do you think would happen? What does *she* want to happen?"

"What do you suppose, Mouse? She wants to get rid of us. Get rid of us or get us to join her coven, like she always wanted."

"She hasn't got a coven, Lynn. She's not even here."

"She's got a witches' coven," Lynn said darkly. "Wherever she is or *what*ever she is, she's trying to build up a cone of power again, trying to get a group of people under her power, just as she tried with Judith and Mother and us. It never stops. It just never seems to stop."

"Maybe boiling her eye did more good than we thought."

"We'll soon know, I suppose," said Lynn. "I wish it was one o'clock. I wish Dad and Mom were home."

Downstairs the clock chimed midnight.

Mouse settled down under the blanket. "I think I'm ready to go to sleep," she murmured.

"I'm not. Do you ever get restless legs?"

"Uh-uh."

"Restless arms?"

"Good night, Lynn."

"Restless head?"

"Go to sleep, Lynn."

For at least a half hour, Lynn tried her best to lie quietly, and when she absolutely had to turn over, she did it as slowly and quietly as possible, making the entire turn in slow motion, inch by inch.

This is ridiculous, she thought. *Maybe I ought to go over in my own bed so I won't wake Mouse up.*

She was just about to get up when she heard a faint noise: *the fluttering.* It seemed to start at the far end of the room, coming closer and closer. At one point it seemed so near to her that Lynn was sure she could reach out and touch it. Her eyes popped wide open and she stared up into the darkness. Almost at once the fluttering began to recede until there was no sound left but the drumming of rain on the roof.

Was it the bat again, Lynn wondered, if it was a bat at all? The same bat that had come into the bedroom the night her father removed the storm windows? She had not heard it for some time, and assumed it had gone out the same way it had come in. Lynn pulled the blanket up over her head, wondering what to do next.

Minutes passed, and then the noise came again, closer still, flying directly past Lynn's ear, scraping against the sheet.

"Mouse!" she said, shaking her friend.

Mouse slumbered on.

What should she do? It seemed selfish to wake her up. Perhaps what Lynn should do was to get up, open the bedroom door, and turn the light on in the hall. Then she could get back in bed, watch, and as soon as she saw the bat fly through the doorway, attracted by the light, she could hurry and close the door again and let her father deal with the bat when he got home. Stevie's door was closed, so it wouldn't bother him.

Slowly Lynn lowered the sheet from her head, thrust one foot out from under the blanket, searching for the floor. Just as she sat up, however, as though it had been lying in wait for her, the noise—the fluttering—came straight at her. This time as it passed, sharp points scratched her cheek, like fingernails, and Lynn screamed.

Mouse sat up like a shot. "What's the matter?"

"S-something's in the room! I think it's a bat."

"Oh, Lordy!"

Before Lynn could stop her, Mouse rolled over, turned on Judith's bedside lamp, and then they saw it—a huge bat, wings spread, coming right at them.

The girls screamed and dived under the covers. Again the creature scratched at the sheet as it passed, the fluttering directly over their ears.

When it stopped circling and the noise quieted, Lynn tried to catch her breath. She could hear the *thump, thump* of her own heart.

"L-Lynn, I never saw a b-bat that big," Mouse whispered.

"Neither did I. It looks horrible! I'm sure it's a bat, though. Listen. Slowly reach out your arm and turn off the lamp. Then I'll get out of bed, go turn on the hall light, and we'll wait for it to fly out. Then we'll close the door."

"I'm too scared."

"It's the only way, Mouse."

Slowly Lynn uncovered her head and looked around. At first she couldn't see it. Then she spotted it on the wall just above Judith's window. It had a long snout, long pointed teeth, and even a long tongue, which it flicked occasionally to one side. There was a growth on its nose that resembled a horseshoe. Mouse finally uncovered her head to look, then quickly covered herself again in terror.

"We c-can't just open the window and get it out of the house?" she whimpered.

"Dad put the screens on last week." Lynn cautiously put one leg over the side of the bed again, eyes on the bat. But Mouse grabbed her.

"Lynn, I hear singing!"

Lynn listened. Now that one foot was on the floor, however, she didn't want to stop. She felt almost desperate to move, to jump, to run. Anything. The strange thing was, *she* couldn't hear the singing.

"What's the song?"

"*You* know! It's that 'Come, my nymphs,' song. Don't go, Lynn!"

Lynn couldn't understand it. She heard nothing at all except the squeak of the springs as she put the other foot on the floor.

Mouse suddenly let go of her arm. "*You're* singing it, Lynn!" She scooted away from her in terror. "*You're* singing that song!"

And then Lynn realized that her lips were moving—her dry, wrinkled lips were forming the words as though she had been humming it to herself all along. At that moment, she heard something else: "Do-*roll*-a!"

"Oh, L-Lordy!" Mouse gasped.

Lynn got slowly out of bed.

"*No*, Lynn!"

"Do-*roll*-a!" the call came again. And it was then that Lynn realized it came from the bat.

As though leading the way, the bat flew to the door of Lynn's room, waiting for her to open it. And trancelike, her dry lips still singing the song, Lynn followed and opened the door.

Suddenly Mouse was on her feet, too, pulling the blanket off the bed, rolling it up in her hand like a sack, and then lunging across the room, swinging the blanket, trying to hit the bat.

The creature circled, swooping low around Mouse's face, wings fluttering menacingly, its beady eyes intent on Lynn.

"Hit it, Lynn!" Mouse cried. "Hit it!"

But Lynn, opening the bedroom door, felt as though her legs belonged to someone else. She moved out into the hallway and started downstairs. She sensed her lips still singing, sensed the bat directly overhead now, then flying ahead of her, leading the way.

"Lynn!" Mouse screamed from the top of the stairs. "Where are you going? Open the back door and maybe it will go out."

Lynn didn't answer. She wanted to tell Mouse that she would. Wanted to say she'd turn on the back porchlight, open the door, and wait until the creature was gone. But even as these thoughts swirled through her mind, she knew she was going outside with the bat. Knew that her feet would take her there.

"Do-roll-a!" the bat called, hovering overhead. And then the words, "Come, my pretty!"

Lynn walked across the kitchen floor in her bare feet and unlatched the door. She stepped out on the screened porch, its floor wet with blowing rain, and unlocked the second door. Rain pummeled against her. The bat flew out and Lynn followed. Down the wet steps and across the soaking grass toward the garden.

She could hear Marjorie calling from the back door. She could feel the wind, the wet, the water—the squish of mud between her toes as her bare feet reached the garden. Against the black of the sky, she could still make out the huge bat, just overhead, circling, waiting for her, leading her on. Once it swooped low and seemed to cackle like an old woman in her ear: "Dorolla, my nymph, my sweet, my pretty."

Weakly Lynn raised one arm to push it away. Her fingers felt stiff, and as she rubbed them together to warm them, they did not feel like her fingers at all—bent and dry and wrinkled with age. Terrified, she ran a finger over her lips. Instead of the smooth skin she was used to feeling, she found deep ridges and furrows. She was no longer herself! She was old! She was . . .

Marjorie's footsteps sounded behind her now, and the closer Mouse came, the more furiously the wind blew, the harder Lynn was pelted with rain. Already her pajamas were plastered against her body like tissue paper.

"Do-*roll*-a!" The voice crooned, "*That's* my pretty! Only a little farther now. Come down to the water, dearie! Come, Dorolla, come!"

As Lynn left the garden and started across the field she could feel her feet sinking ankle deep in mud. Already she could hear the roar of water in Cowden's Creek as it overflowed its banks.

She could not tell where Mouse was because the wind was howling so, and drowned out every sound but the persistent calling: "Come, Dorolla—to the water, dearie!"

Lynn made a conscious effort to stop, but she could not even feel her legs now, as though her whole body was numb. She seemed to have nothing but ears that were working—listening to the call and obeying.

She thought she heard Mouse somewhere behind her, but her eyes tried to focus on the water ahead. In the blackness of the night she could just make out the handrails of the little footbridge that crossed the creek. The floor of the bridge itself was underwater. Lynn could not tell where she was supposed to cross and then she knew that she was not to cross at all, but to go on into the water.

"Do-*roll*-a!" the voice came still again.

"M-Mouse! Help me!" Lynn managed to cry as she started down into the creek—the water up to her calves, then her knees, her thighs. "It's the eye! Grab the eye!"

There was a splash behind her, and then she felt a hand on her arm. At the same time, a powerful gust of wind almost knocked her over, but the hand held her up. The hand became two hands, then two arms.

"Give it to me, Lynn! Give me the eye!" Mouse was saying.

But Lynn could not. She felt very weak, very old. Her legs seemed to buckle as the water swirled around her, and she leaned against her friend. She felt Mouse's hand searching her pajama top, her pocket. Then fingers inside the pocket. Finally, as she struggled against the current, Mouse's arm around her, Lynn saw, through the darkness, Mouse draw back her arm and fling the eye as hard as she could out into the churning water.

For a moment both girls continued to stand in the creek, holding on to each other, the rain hitting at them, the wind howling, and above the roar of the water there came a hideous screech—part bird, part bat, part woman, part witch.

Instantly both girls turned, leaped out of the water, slogged back across the muddy field, then the garden, then the yard, hair and eyelashes matted with water, pajamas drenched and clinging to their bodies.

(Note: "The Witch's Eye" is taken from Chapters 14 and 15 of *The Witch's Eye*.)

Charles J. Finger

THE MAGIC BALL

COLD-EYED witch lived in the Cordilleras and when the first snow commenced to fall she was always full of glee, standing on a rock, screaming like a wind-gale and rubbing her hands. For it pleased her to see the winter moon, the green country blotted out, the valleys white, the trees snow-laden, and the waters ice-bound and black. Winter was her hunting time and her eating time, and in the summer she slept. So she was full of a kind of savage joy when there were leaden clouds and drifting gales, and she waited and watched, waited and watched, ever ready to spring upon frost-stiffened creatures that went wandering down to the warmer lowlands.

This witch was a wrinkled creature, hard of eye, thin-lipped, with hands that looked like roots of trees, and so tough was her skin that knife could not cut nor arrow pierce it. In the country that swept down to the sea she was greatly feared, and hated, too. The hate came because by some strange magic she was able to draw children to her one by one, and how she did it no man knew. But the truth is that she had a magic ball, a ball bright and shining and of many colours, and this she left in places where children played, but never where man or woman could see it.

One day, near the lake called Oretta, a brother and sister were at play and saw the magic ball at the foot of a little hill. Pleased with its brightness and beauty Natalia ran to it, intending to pick it up and take it home, but, to her surprise, as she drew near to it the ball rolled away; then, a little way off, came to rest again. Again she ran to it and almost had her hand on it when it escaped, exactly as a piece of thistle-down does, just as she was about to grasp it. So she followed it, always seeming to be on the point of catching it but never doing so, and as she ran her brother Luis followed, careful lest she should come to harm. The strange part of it was that every time the ball stopped it rested close to some berry bush or by the edge of a crystal-clear spring, so that she, like all who were thus led away, always found at the moment of resting something to eat or to drink or to refresh herself. Nor, strangely enough, did she tire, but because of the magic went skipping and running and jumping just as long as she followed the ball. Nor did any one under the spell of that magic note the passing of time, for days were like hours and a night like the shadow of a swiftly flying cloud.

At last, chasing the ball, Natalia and Luis came to a

place in the valley where the Río Chico runs between great hills, and it was dark and gloomy and swept by heavy gray clouds. The land was strewn with mighty broken rocks and here and there were patches of snow, and soon great snow flakes appeared in the air. Then boy and girl were terror-struck, for they knew with all the wandering and twisting and turning they had lost their way. But the ball still rolled on, though slower now, and the children followed. But the air grew keener and colder and the sun weaker, so that they were very glad indeed when they came to a black rock where, at last, the ball stopped.

Natalia picked it up, and for a moment gazed at its beauty, but for a moment only. For no sooner had she gazed at it and opened her lips to speak than it vanished as a soap bubble does, at which her grief was great. Luis tried to cheer her and finding that her hands were icy cold led her to the north side of the rock where it was warmer, and there he found a niche like a lap between two great arms, and in the moss-grown cranny Natalia coiled herself up and was asleep in a minute. As for Luis, knowing that as soon as his sister had rested they must set out about finding a way home, he sat down intending to watch. But not very long did he keep his eyes open, for he was weary and sad at heart. He tried hard to keep awake, even holding his eyelids open with his fingers, and he stared hard at a sunlit hilltop across the valley, but even that seemed to make him sleepy. Then, too, there were slowly nodding pine trees and the whispering of leaves, coming in a faint murmur from the mountainside. So, soon, Luis slept.

Natalia, being out of the blustering wind, was very comfortable in the little niche between the great stone arms, and she dreamed that she was at home. Her mother, she thought, was combing her hair and singing as she did so. So she forgot her hunger and weariness, and in her dreamland knew nothing of the bare black rocks and snow-patched hills. Instead, she seemed to be at home where the warm firelight danced on the walls and lighted her father's brown face to a lively red as he mended his horse gear. She saw her brother, too, with his jet-black hair and cherry-red lips. But her mother, she thought, grew rough and careless and pulled her hair, so that she gave a little cry of pain and awoke. Then in a flash she knew where she was and was chilled to the bone with the piercing wind that swept down from the mountain top. Worse still, in front of her stood the old witch of the hills, pointing, pointing, pointing with knotty forefinger, and there were nails on her hands and feet that looked like claws.

Natalia tried to rise, but could not, and her heart was like stone when she found what had happened. It was this: while she slept, the witch had stroked and combed her hair, and meanwhile wrought magic, so that the girl's hair was grown into the rock so very close that she could not as much as turn her head. All that she could do was to stretch forth her arms, and when she saw Luis a little way off she called to him most piteously. But good Luis made no move. Instead, he stood with arms wide apart like one who feels a wall in the dark, moving his hands this way and that. Then Natalia wept, not understanding and little knowing that the witch had bound Luis with a spell, so that there seemed to be an invisible wall around the rock through which he could not pass, try as he would. But he heard the witch singing in her high and cracked voice, and this is what she sang:

> *"Valley all pebble-sown,*
> *Valley where wild winds moan!*
> *Come, mortals, come.*
>
> *"Valley so cool and white,*
> *Valley of winter night,*
> *Come, children, come.*
>
> *"Straight like a shaft to mark,*
> *Come they to cold and dark,*
> *Children of men!"*

Then she ceased and stood with her root-like finger upraised, and from near by came the voice of a great white owl, which took up the song, saying:

> *"Things of the dark and things without name,*
> *Save us from light and the torch's red flame."*

Now all this was by starlight, but the moment the owl had ceased, from over the hill came a glint of light as the pale moon rose, and with a sound like a thunderclap the witch melted into the great rock and the owl flapped away heavily.

"Brother," whispered the girl, "you heard what the owl said?"

"Yes, sister, I heard," he answered.

"Brother, come to me. I am afraid," said Natalia, and commenced to cry a little.

"Sister," he said, "I try but I cannot. There is something through which I cannot pass. I can see but I cannot press through."

"Can you not climb over, dear Luis?" asked Natalia.

"No, Natalia. I have reached high as I can, but the wall that I cannot see goes up and up."

"Is there no way to get in on the other side of the rock, dear, dear Luis? I am very cold and afraid, being here alone."

"Sister, I have walked around. I have felt high and low. But it is always the same. I cannot get through, I cannot climb over, I cannot crawl under. But I shall stay here with you, so fear not."

At that Natalia put her hands to her face and wept a little, but very quietly, and it pained Luis to see the tears roll down her cheeks and turn to little ice pearls as they fell. After a while Natalia spoke again, but through sobs.

"Brother mine, you heard what the owl said?"

"Yes, sister."

"Does it mean nothing to you?" she asked.

"Nothing," he replied.

"But listen," said Natalia. "These were the words: 'Save us from light and the torch's red flame.' "

"I heard that, Natalia. What does it mean?"

"It means, brother, that the things in this horrible valley fear fire. So go, brother. Leave me a while but find fire, coming back with it swiftly. There will be sickening loneliness, so haste, haste."

Hearing that, Luis was sad, for he was in no mood to leave his sister in that plight. Still she urged him, saying: "Speed, brother, speed."

Even then he hesitated, until with a great swoop there passed over the rock a condor wheeling low, and it said as it passed: "Fire will conquer frosted death."

"You hear, brother," said Natalia. "So speed and find fire and return before night."

Then Luis stayed no longer, but waved his sister a farewell and set off down the valley, following the condor that hovered in the air, now darting away and now returning. So Luis knew that the great bird led him, and he ran, presently finding the river and following it until he reached the great vega where the waters met.

At the meeting of the waters he came to a house, a poor thing made of earth and stones snuggled in a warm fold of the hills. No one was about there, but as the condor flew high and, circling in the air, became a small speck, Luis knew that it would be well to stay a while and see what might befall. Pushing open the door he saw by the ashes in the fireplace that someone lived there, for there were red embers well covered to keep the fire alive. So seeing that the owner of the house would return soon, he made himself free of the place, which was the way of that country, and brought fresh water from the spring. Then he gathered wood and piled it neatly by the fireside. Next he blew upon the embers and added twigs and sticks until a bright fire glowed, after which he took the broom of twigs and swept the earth floor clean.

How the man of the house came into the room Luis

never knew, but there he was, sitting by the fire on a stool. He looked at things but said nothing to Luis, only nodding his head. Then he brought bread and yerba and offered some to Luis. After they had eaten the old man spoke, and this is what he said:

"Wicked is the white witch, and there is but one way to defeat her. What, lad, is the manner of her defeat? Tell me that."

Then Luis, remembering what the condor had said, repeated the words: " 'Fire will conquer frosted death.' "

"True," said the man slowly, nodding his head. "And your sister is there. Now here comes our friend the condor, who sees far and knows much."

> *"Now with cold grows faint her breath,*
> *Fire will conquer frosted death."*

Having said that the great bird wheeled up sharply.

But no sooner was it out of sight than a turkey came running and stood a moment, gobbling. To it the old man gave a lighted brand, repeating the words the condor had spoken.

Off sped the turkey with the blazing stick, running through marsh and swamp in a straight line, and Luis and the old man watched. Soon the bird came to a shallow lagoon, yet made no halt. Straight through the water it sped, and so swiftly that the spray dashed up on either side. High the turkey held the stick, but not high enough, for the splashing water quenched the fire, and seeing that, the bird returned, dropping the blackened stick at the old man's feet.

"Give me another, for the maiden is quivering cold," said the turkey. "This time I will run around the lake."

"No. No," answered the man. "You must know that when the water spirit kisses the fire king, the fire king dies. So, that you may remember, from now and for ever you will carry on your feathers the marks of rippling water."

Down again swooped the condor and a little behind him came a goose, flying heavily. As before, the condor cried:

"Now with cold grows faint her breath,
Fire will conquer frosted death,"

then flew away again toward the witch mountain.

To the goose the old man gave a blazing stick and at once the brave bird set off, flying straight in the direction the condor had taken. Over vega and over lagoon she went, pausing only at a snowclad hilltop, because the stick had burned close to her beak. So she dropped it in the snow to get a better hold, and when she picked it up again there was but a charred thing. Sad enough the goose returned to the house, bearing the blackened stick, and begged to be given another chance.

"No. No," said the old man. "The silver snow queen's kiss is death to the fire king. That is something you must remember. From now on and for ever you must carry feathers of gray like the ashes. But here comes the condor and we must hear his message."

Sadly then the goose went away, her feathers ash gray, and the condor wheeled low again, calling:

---

*"Fainter grows the maiden's breath,
Night must bring the frosted death,"*

and having said, like an arrow he shot off.

No sooner had he gone than the long-legged, long-billed flamingo dropped to the ground.

"Your beak is long," said the old man, "but fly swiftly, for the stick is short."

The flamingo took the burning stick by the end and made straight for the mountain, racing with all possible speed. As for Luis, he made up his mind to tarry no longer and set off, running like a deer. But an ostrich, seeing him, spread her wings like sails and ran by his side. On her back Luis placed his hand, and with that help sped as fast as the flamingo. In the air the flamingo went like an arrow, resting not, although the blazing fire burned her neck and breast until it became pink and red. But that she heeded not. Straight up the valley and to the rock where Natalia was bound went she, and into a heap of dried moss on the south side of the rock she dropped the blazing stick. Up leaped the dancing flames, and with a tremendous noise the rock flew into a thousand pieces and the power of the witch was gone for ever. As for Natalia, she was at once freed, and with her gentle, cool hand stroked the breast of the flamingo so that the burns were healed, but as a sign of its bravery the bird has carried a crimson breast from that day to this.

As for Natalia and Luis, they lived for many, many years in the valley, and about them birds of many kinds played and lived and reared their young, and the magic ball of the witch lived only in the memory of men.

Paul Fleischman

THE MAN OF
INFLUENCE

1

LIGHTNING TWITCHED like a dreaming dog's legs. The wind blew. Rain fell. And Zorelli lay awake in the night.

Wide-eyed, he listened to the beating rain, enduring each drop that struck the roof. He turned toward Marta, his wife, beside him. She was sleeping soundly, unaware of the weather, and he gazed at her with contempt. He himself had never found it possible to sleep on a rainy night.

Rain, after all, was the enemy of stone, pounding it finally into dust. And Zorelli was a stone carver by trade, a maker of monuments.

·   ·   ·

"Lolling in the doorway, letting in the cold." Marta looked up from scrubbing the floor, sighed wearily, and shook her head. "Come now, Zorelli—will that keep us fed?"

The sculptor ignored her and surveyed the sky, while his cat, Angelina, coiled about his ankles. The storm had passed over the rooftops of Genoa. The cobblestones glistened and the morning air was filled with the gaudy crowing of roosters.

"Is this any way to lure a patron?" Marta pleaded with her husband. "Unshaven, dressed in a filthy tunic, lurking about the doorway like a thief?"

A pair of mounted soldiers rode by. A fruit seller passed, pushing his cart. Zorelli looked down at Angelina, who cried and rubbed meaningfully against his legs. Stepping inside, he searched the kitchen and fed her the last scrap of cheese in the house.

"That cat of yours never lacks for food—but what of us?" asked Marta. "Already the mice have deserted the house. By tomorrow night we'll have nothing to gnaw on—unless, of course, you pick up your hammer and carve us a roast goose out of granite."

Zorelli glared at her in silence, then turned and stormed into his studio.

Restlessly, he paced the room. He was a powerful man, broad shouldered, proud chinned, and he settled himself at last on a stool, took note of the spotless floor, and sneered. It should have been littered with chips of stone. There ought to have been granite dust in the air. But commerce was bad, Genoa's harbor was still, and the mighty Boccas and Tarentinos, whose fleeting features Zorelli had transferred to statues of imperishable stone, no longer had money to spare for his skills. Even the ruling Ferrantes, his grandest patrons, seemed to have forgotten him.

In disgust, he gazed at his idle tools. If no commission came his way today he'd be forced to return to work at the quarry, toiling once again beside his loutish father and his foul-smelling brothers. And yet, Zorelli reflected, he was an intimate of the high-born now. He'd strolled down the halls of the cultured and rich, arranged them in poses, engaged them in talk. He jumped to his feet and strode outside, shuddering to think of descending once more to the coarse, sweaty company of the quarry.

Aimlessly, he roamed the town, walking briskly in the chill autumn air. Down a side street he caught a glimpse of the plaza and his mounted statue of Lorenzo Ferrante, Governor of Genoa, her leader in arms and great patron of culture. Zorelli paused, then marched ahead, savoring his link with the man.

He entered the swarming marketplace—and erupted in a rage when a man bumped him in passing. After all, he was no worthless commoner like the rest—his customers were persons of influence. His wares were no melons or stinking fish, but immortality itself!

He picked his way through the motley gathering. Vendors bellowed, pigs squealed. Beggars and thieves circulated like maggots. Zorelli struggled to escape the crowd, when all of a sudden a shout rang out. Chickens scattered, the throng parted, and Lorenzo himself, mounted on his steed, solemnly entered the market.

At last! thought Zorelli, straining for a view. In the midst of the rabble—a man worthy of stone!

Genoa's governor towered above the crowd, peering ahead with hawklike aloofness. Gazing in reverence upon the great man, Zorelli noticed his black cloak and hat and knew he must be bound for the grave of his nephew, the infant Alessandro, to pay his yearly respects. Zorelli himself had carved the tomb for the child, who would have ruled the house of Ferrante, and therefore Genoa itself, had a window been shut and the prince not taken a chill one night and died.

Grimly, Lorenzo rode through the market. Zorelli longed to catch his attention, to be acknowledged and elevated above the rest. Like a sunflower, he slowly turned, devotedly facing Lorenzo as he passed, while the object of his veneration stared ahead, unaware of his presence.

Once again the noisy bargaining resumed. Scornfully, Zorelli regarded the crowd.

Mayflies! he swore. Creatures of a day! Never would their paltry lives earn preservation in stone!

He threaded his way through the multitude, stopping to watch two women haggle with a vendor over the price of a fish.

Beasts! hissed Zorelli. Concerned only with eating!

With relief he fled the marketplace, exalted with his lofty perspective. And yet—he passed a bakery and inhaled the scent of freshly baked bread—he too felt a sudden pang of hunger.

Cursing his stomach, he emptied his pockets to pay for a roll and stormed away.

·   ·   ·

That night Zorelli paced his studio long after Marta had climbed into bed. A restlessness grew up inside him whenever he wasn't swinging his hammer or exerting his files against stone.

He made up his mind to take a walk, stepped outside, and headed for the harbor. Angelina followed behind him.

"The night is black, is it not, Angelina?" The sculptor's cat was black as well and had disappeared upon entering the darkness like a fish thrown back to sea.

"The moon has yet to rise," said Zorelli. "But we know our way about, don't we now?"

Invisibly, Angelina followed beside him. It was late and they were alone in the streets. Gradually the salt air grew stronger, and soon the two of them reached the docks and wandered out to the end of a wharf.

"The waters are still tonight, Angelina." The waves lapped softly against the wharf. The few boats at anchor bobbed peacefully. Angelina sat and peered out to sea, sniffing the air with interest.

"And the stars!" The sculptor gazed up at the heavens. "Have you ever before beheld them so bright?"

"Never!" came a voice in reply.

At once Angelina hissed and fled. Zorelli whirled—and found himself facing the flickering image of what seemed to be a man.

"A pox on the stars!" continued the voice. *"Too* bright for my liking. Aye, blinding, they are!"

Zorelli studied the speaker in wonder. He was short legged and burly and missing an ear. Fitfully, he glowed and dimmed, as if he were made of starlight himself.

"You're Zorelli, the stone carver, if I'm not mistaken." His clothes were ragged and glimmered like their wearer, as if they were but the dying embers of their former selves.

"And who—or what—are you?" asked Zorelli.

"What *am* I?" The apparition snorted. "Why, a ghost! What *else* did you take me for?"

Zorelli stared at the spirit in awe, his hands fluttering like moths. He wondered where Angelina had gone, and had he not been trapped at the end of the wharf he would gladly have fled as well.

"And what brings you—here?" the sculptor stammered.

"What *brings* me here," said the specter, "is you."

Zorelli stiffened. "What is it you want?"

"Your services, naturally."

"What?" gasped Zorelli.

"I want to hire you. To fashion a statue."

Zorelli gaped at the ghost in amazement.

"I'm prepared to pay, you understand." He reached into a pocket and produced a coin purse.

"Twenty-five ducats now. Aye, and fifty more when you're finished."

Zorelli's eyes lit. Seventy-five ducats! No more would he have to return to the quarry! He could live for months on such a sum. And yet—he found himself staring at the coin purse.

"How can I be sure that the money—is real?"

The specter grinned and shook the purse, causing the coins to jingle brightly in proof of their substantiality.

Zorelli smiled. "Well now!" he spoke up. "And what

manner of statue had you in mind? Something for a garden? A nymph, perhaps?"

The spirit peered into the stone carver's eyes. "I would have you carve the statue of me."

"Of *you?*" Zorelli froze in astonishment. He stared at the specter shimmering before him, a quantity of phosphorescence poured in the mold of a man.

"Naturally, I'm accustomed to dealing—with the living." Zorelli fumbled awkwardly. With growing revulsion he took note of the spirit's missing ear, his crooked teeth, and the long jagged rip down the front of his doublet. Had warm flesh belonged to him he might have been taken for a beggar, or a rag merchant dressed in his wares, and suddenly Zorelli wondered if the man was worthy of salvation in stone—or deserved forgetting, like most of humanity.

The sculptor turned his eyes toward the water.

"If I might be so bold," he asked delicately, "were you a man of any—*influence* while you lived?"

"I'm afraid I was," answered the specter.

Zorelli jerked in surprise—and relief. The man was of more account than appeared. Stone would not be misused.

"I—thought as much," mumbled the sculptor. He felt embarrassed at having asked the question and was flooded with a sudden respect for the spirit.

"Then again," said the ghost, "if you don't have the time—"

"Not at all!" Zorelli interrupted. "I should be honored, of course, to accept the task. Why, sitting at home I've a fine block of marble—what size of a statue had you in mind?"

"Life-size," the spirit answered gravely. "I wish to be shown just as I was."

"Fine!" The stone carver beamed at having found himself a patron at last. "Naturally I'll dress you in the finest attire, whatever you—"

"No need for that," spoke the phantom. "I want to be shown in the clothes I have on. Aye, just as I looked that night."

Zorelli gaped at the ghost's worn-out shoes, wretched doublet, and rat-gnawed cap. "A man of influence dressed— in rags? Surely a fine, turbaned hat at the least—"

"As for the pose," continued the ghost, "see that you show me cradling an infant. Aye, and holding a cup to its lips."

Zorelli digested his words in dismay. He was accustomed to depicting his subjects triumphant, with swords upraised, in the midst of great deeds. But a man—feeding an infant in his arms?

The sculptor tried to compose himself. "Your child, of course—"

"Not at all," barked the spirit. "And at my feet, carve out a cat. Scrawny, with no left ear—just like me."

Zorelli started.

"A true friend, he was. Found him here by the water one winter, and as soon as I saw he was missing an ear— why, I knew we'd understand each other, and get along just fine."

Zorelli stood facing his patron, dumbfounded. His earlier enthusiasm had left, replaced by a strange unease.

"Of course, I'll need to sketch you," he said, as if hoping

to talk the ghost out of the project. "Make studies and drawings, you understand."

The spirit noticed the rising moon and seemed anxious
to retreat from its light.

"Tomorrow night, then. Here. The same time."

He handed the coin purse to Zorelli, who opened it
quickly to inspect the money. By the time he'd assured himself and looked up, his patron had disappeared.

2

The sun rose, devouring the frost on the ground, and
Zorelli rolled out of bed.

Suddenly he remembered the ghost. He wondered if he
had dreamed of the meeting. Then he reached for his tunic—
and plucked out the coin purse.

He darted to a window and examined the coins. They
were gold. He weighed one in his hand. It seemed to be real
enough.

He hid the purse, then rushed out the door and down the
street to a bakery.

"A loaf of bread!" the sculptor called out, above the din
of the other customers.

A sow-faced baker fetched him a loaf. Cautiously, the
stone carver held out one of the coins he'd received from the
spirit—and watched in wonder as the man snatched it up,
quickly returned him his change, and moved on.

For a moment Zorelli stood there, speechless, staring at
the coins in his palm.

"And what's the matter with you?" snapped the baker. "A complaint with my counting?"

"Not at all!" said Zorelli.

"Step aside, then! Let the customers through!"

Smiling to himself, Zorelli scurried home.

"And where did you get money for bread?" asked Marta, eyeing the loaf in amazement.

Zorelli hungrily tore off a hunk. "Just where you would expect!" he replied. "I'm a sculptor. And I've been engaged by a patron!"

Victoriously, he marched into his studio.

"A patron?" Marta called after him. "Who?"

Zorelli stopped. She would never believe him.

"A man," he faltered. "A man—of some note."

He turned, relieved to find her absorbed in devouring a chunk of bread. Looking down at the piece in his own hand, he marveled that something so dense and substantial had resulted from so airy a being.

The sculptor filled his belly with bread, then sharpened his chisels one by one. He inspected his mallets, his rasps, his rifflers, his gouges and points, compass and square. Reverently, he cleaned his tools, then struggled with the block of marble, sliding it into the center of the room.

He gazed at it, patiently searching it for the proper pose of man, child, and cat. In his eyes the stone lost its solidity. It was fluid as quicksilver, a river of shapes. Pensively, he walked around it. From his stool, he stared at it for hours. He regarded it from near and far. And he waited for darkness to come.

·   ·   ·

"No shortage of stars in the sky tonight!"

Zorelli spun around. Down the wharf came the spirit, flickering as if concocted of fireflies.

"Aye, they pain my eyes, they do! If I had me a long-handled candle snuffer, such as would reach—why, I'd put 'em all out. Believe me I would—and hang a cloak on the moon!"

Zorelli stared at him, awed afresh to find himself in the employ of what was nothing more than the residue of a life, a cloud of ash, a burnt wick of a man.

"You wanted to draw me," spat out the ghost. "And I'm here. So let's get on with it!"

The waters whispered. A sea gull squawked. Zorelli produced parchment and charcoal and commenced to sketch, by his subject's own light.

He eyed the ghost's teeth, crooked and sparse, leaning like tombstones in a forgotten graveyard. With mounting unease, he duly recorded his broken nose and the scar down his throat, longing for the smooth skins and noble features to which he was accustomed.

"As for your—ear," he spoke up with difficulty. "Naturally a hat, tilted to one side—"

"Never! I won't have you covering it up. I want to be exposed for just what I am. Or rather, for what I *was*—that night."

Distastefully Zorelli sketched the ear, hurrying over its ragged border.

"Seventeen years it's been that way." The spirit gazed out over the harbor. "Aye, since I first took up with the Boccas."

The Boccas! Zorelli brightened at the name. Spice mer-chants, they were, wealthy and refined. Zorelli himself had carved busts of the children, and he swelled with a sudden respect for his patron, as for all who lived in the world of the great.

"You were associated with the Boccas?" he asked.

"I should say! Seven years I served 'em."

Zorelli sketched the ghost's tattered doublet, wishing he could ignore the ragged tear that ran down the front.

"In what—*capacity* did you serve?" grinned the stone carver. "That is, if I may presume to ask."

"Commerce," said the ghost.

"Commerce?"

"That's right." He fingered his ear. "So to speak."

Zorelli wondered at his patron's meaning but hesitated to press him further.

"Aye, but that was long ago," the spirit mused, scanning the water. "Even before I'd met Tarentino."

"The Tarentinos, of course!" beamed Zorelli. He'd once carved a statue of Vito Tarentino, the government diplomat.

"A family of means," boasted the sculptor. "And magnif-icent learning as well!"

He sketched his patron's stumpy legs, imperceptibly lengthening them, as befitted a personage of his evident rank.

"It was the old man—Vito—I worked for," said the spirit. "Back when he was stationed in Florence."

"Truly!" Zorelli gawked, impressed. "And what, if I might ask, was your work?"

"Matters of state," the ghost answered back.

"Really, now."

"Right," said the spirit. "In a matter of speaking, you understand."

Zorelli sketched the ghost's battered shoes, pondering his words. To whom was he offering shelter in stone? Trembling, he regarded the ghost's tattered outfit, his broken nose and unsettling ear, and wished he'd never accepted his gold. But what was he to do—return to the quarry? After all, the spirit claimed to have been a man of influence while he'd lived, a point to which Zorelli clung like a cat.

"When can you have it finished?" asked the ghost.

"A month," Zorelli replied. "At the soonest."

"Fine!" He fingered the rip in his doublet. "Aye, a great relief it'll be. Just remember—down at my feet, a cat. One eared, and looking up at me. I want him to see for himself. See it plain."

Zorelli rolled up his sheet of parchment.

"When it's done," said the ghost, "put it in a wagon and take the road to Rompoli, by night."

The ghost set off.

"But wait!" cried Zorelli. "Where do I deliver it—and what of the payment? The other fifty ducats you promised!"

"I'll meet you along the way," said the spirit, and disappeared down the wharf.

3

Outside Zorelli's door, sun followed storm. The trees dropped their leaves. Voices passed by. Of these, however, he remained unaware. The statue alone absorbed his attention.

All day and deep into the nights he labored, working by sunlight, then candles and lamps. He joyed in stretching his muscles again, exulted in swinging his ringing hammer. Streams of sweat ran down his throat as if he were stoking the sun's own fires, and when he could work no more he fell into bed, exhausted and satisfied.

"What's your opinion, Angelina?" the sculptor addressed his cat one day. He glanced from her to the cat he was carving. "A fine beginning, wouldn't you say?"

Zorelli stepped back and studied the statue. The stocky form of the ghost had emerged, but the cat still lay hidden within the marble. The stone clung to the figure like a fog, and the sculptor reached for a chisel, took up his hammer, and returned to dispersing it.

"Tell me, Angelina," said Zorelli. "Have you ever seen such a statue before?"

The cat remained still, asleep in the sun.

"Never!" replied Marta, looking on from the doorway.

She stepped into the studio and eyed the marble. "A statue—commissioned by a beggar in rags?"

Zorelli swallowed. "Marta, I assure you—"

"What then—a thief? Or a murderer, perhaps?" She smiled knowingly at her husband. "Do you take me for a fool? No such patron exists! Amusing yourself in marble, you are—and *stealing* the money you give me for food."

"Marta, let me explain—"

"Explain?" She glared at the stone carver acidly. "All that I need to have explained is what possessed you to carve such a figure—and ruin a perfectly good block of marble!"

She swept out of the room, leaving the sculptor contemplating the statue and its subject.

Never, he mused, had he carved such a face. The barbarous mouth was that of a cutthroat. The eyes belonged to a hangman—or his prey. With each hammer blow he grew more afraid of the figure gradually being revealed.

And yet, Zorelli reminded himself, the man was acquainted with the wealthy Boccas, and the cultured Tarentinos as well. And he certainly hadn't lacked for money. Perhaps, he reasoned, *all* ghosts looked as grubby as this one—even the ghosts of the great.

He tried to drive the specter from his mind, picked up his hammer, and returned to work, musing on the power he possessed to fix the world's memory on a man for the length of the life of stone. Pounding, scraping, sanding, polishing, he gloried afresh in his ability to rescue his subjects from oblivion, securing for himself, parasitelike, a portion of their immortality.

Day by day the hammers became lighter, the chisels smaller, the files finer. Chipping gave way to grinding, then sanding, each tool removing the marks of its predecessor.

And then, one day, the statue was finished.

"Tell me—what do you think, Angelina?" Zorelli picked her up and approached the figure who held a cup to an infant, watched by a one-eared cat. "Come now, let me hear your opinion."

Desperately, she jumped from his arms.

That afternoon the stone carver hired a pair of horses and a wagon, and with the help of three other brawny men loaded the statue into the back. When evening fell, he snapped the reins and headed down the road to Rompoli.

The night was still, the wintry air bare. The sky overhead was littered with stars. For an hour he drove among frost-stricken fields, wondering just where it was he was headed—when suddenly he sighted a shimmer ahead.

"Well met!" grinned the ghost, approaching the wagon. "You brought the statue, then?"

"There in the back."

"Fine!" beamed the spirit. "Finally! Aye, a great relief it'll be."

He climbed aboard, glowing unreally, as if he were but a magician's illusion.

"How much farther?" Zorelli asked.

"Oh, we've a bit of a ways," smiled the spirit.

Zorelli gave the reins a shake, sharing none of his patron's good cheer. He glanced at the ghost's filthy attire and shuddered at the thought of how his patron must have stunk while he was alive. Even in stone such a man would draw flies. And yet, he claimed to have been of some importance. . . .

"You mentioned before your connection with the Boccas," Zorelli spoke up hesitantly. "Engaged in the spice commerce, didn't you say?"

"That's right," his companion answered back.

"Master of the countinghouse, were you? Or captain of a ship, perhaps?" The sculptor smiled hopefully.

"Not likely. The competition was my job."

"The competition?"

"Right," said the spirit. "Making sure no other pesky traders reached port with a load of pepper before us." He reached absently for his missing ear. "And trying to stay alive in the bargain."

The smile deserted Zorelli's lips. He studied the specter. Was he speaking of foul play? Naturally, he'd heard of such things—but the polished Boccas? The thought was absurd.

Nervously Zorelli clutched the reins, guiding the wagon down the road toward its unknown destination.

"I recall that you mentioned working with Vito Tarentino as well," he spoke up. "Employed in matters of state, I believe."

"Aye, matters of state," said the ghost.

Zorelli smiled respectfully. "Of what sort—if I may be so bold?"

"Finding out," said the spirit matter-of-factly.

"Finding out?"

"That's right," the ghost replied. "Whatever the old man wanted to know. Listening behind doors, searching rooms, paying the servants for what they knew. Aye, he kept me busy, he did."

Zorelli stared at the specter in shock. Tarentino, the renowned thinker and statesman—secretly engaging spies? Surely this mist of a man was lying. And yet, the sculptor asked himself, why should a ghost depart from the truth?

"Turn off to the left there," commanded the spirit. "Aye, that's where my poor bones be."

"Your bones?" said Zorelli. "Why here, of all places?"

"*I* wasn't consulted in the matter," snapped the ghost.

Zorelli guided the horses off the road and into a rocky meadow.

"Dead ahead, there. Aye, that's the spot."

The wagon banged and bounced over the ground, till Zorelli brought it at last to a halt.

"Fine!" exclaimed the spirit, hopping down. "The earth being soft as it is from the rains, I thought you could tip out the statue feet first and let it plant itself in the ground."

Zorelli climbed into the bed of the wagon, anxious to be rid of the statue and its subject. He breathed in deeply, and with the sum of his strength shoved the sculpture along the bed till it teetered, swung upright, and plunged into the earth.

"Well done," cheered the spirit. "Well done, indeed." Smiling, he studied the statue before him, running his fingers over the forms.

"Perfect!" he whispered. "Already I can feel it!" Blissfully, he gazed at the marble.

"Is this to be—your gravestone?" asked Zorelli.

"In a manner of speaking," murmured the spirit. He reached into a pocket, pulled out a coin purse, and handed it to Zorelli.

"The rest of your payment. You'll find it all there."

Zorelli watched, flattered and awed, as the ghost returned his gaze to the statue. Mounting the wagon and grabbing the reins, the sculptor felt suddenly loath to leave.

"If I might ask but one question," Zorelli spoke up. "Why was it you wished to be shown feeding an infant?"

The spirit turned. "I wasn't *feeding* the tyke." He fixed his eyes on the stone carver. "On the contrary, I was murdering it."

"Murdering?" gasped Zorelli.

"That's right. The cup I put to its lips held poison."

Zorelli stared at the ghost, speechless. He felt suddenly weak. His hands took to trembling. A *murderer*—celebrated in stone? Stone that he, Zorelli, had carved?

"Whatever—possessed you," stammered the sculptor, "to pay to have such a scene depicted?"

The specter smiled. "A peaceful sleep. I was murdered myself, you see, that same night. Before I had time to get home to my cat and properly confess my crime."

Zorelli's thoughts whirled. "The cat?"

"That's right." The spirit's eyes brightened. "The one you carved. Oh, he was a fine companion, and whenever I did something that troubled my sleep—why, I told him about it. Aye, and slept sound."

Zorelli's gaze rested on the cat, then slowly traveled up the statue.

"And the infant?" he faltered, struggling with the words.

"Just six months old. Alessandro, they called him."

"His full name!" the stone carver demanded, determined to know the full truth of the crime.

"Alessandro Ferrante."

The sculptor paled. "Lorenzo's nephew?"

"Aye, that's him."

"Impossible!" Zorelli jumped to the ground. "He died of a cold! A chill in the night! I carved the tomb for the child myself!"

The specter snorted. "A chill, was it now?" He grinned, revealing his crooked teeth. "It was Lorenzo himself who paid me to do it. Paid me those ducats I gave to you." He glanced at the rip down the front of his doublet. "And him who had me stabbed, as well."

In disbelief, Zorelli plucked out the coin purse and gaped at it in horror.

"Lorenzo Ferrante?" he murmured hypnotically. Wide-eyed, the stone carver stared at the coin purse, begging to disbelieve his own words.

"Aye," the ghost chuckled. "That's the one."

Zorelli stood motionless. He felt chilled and stiff, as if his own flesh were turning to stone.

Slowly, he climbed back onto the wagon and settled his gaze on the ghost. This then was his claim to influence, the sculptor numbly realized—to have made Lorenzo master of Genoa. Dazed and disoriented, Zorelli finally took up the reins, shook them, and left the ghost behind.

As if spellbound, the stone carver bounced along. While he entered Genoa the moon rose in the east, illuminating the Boccas' mansion, before which Zorelli paused awhile. It lit the Tarentinos' villa as well, where the sculptor halted once again. He passed the fine homes of his other fine patrons, then brought the wagon to a stop at the plaza. In the stillness he gazed at his statue of Lorenzo, astride his steed, glowing in the moonlight.

Shaking the reins, he drove on to the harbor. And there the sculptor climbed down from the wagon, shuffled out to the end of a wharf, and dropped the coin purse into the sea.

Ruing stone's durability, he scanned the horizon, and smiled to see clouds. Then he turned around, walked back to the wagon, mounted, and urged the horses homeward. And that night Zorelli the stone carver fervently prayed for rain.

E. L. Konigsburg

CAMP FAT

OUR CAMP had an Indian name just like every other camp in the mountains, but we called it Camp Fat. And so did every other camp in the mountains.

Sarah was going to music camp. Linda to arts and crafts, Gloria was going to science camp and Fay to water sports. When they asked me where I was going, I told them *regular camp*. Sarah said that she didn't believe me, and Linda said that she didn't either because there was no such thing as regular camp. I asked them where they thought regular kids went, and they said that regular kids didn't ever go to camp.

The day I left, my mother said, "Clara, inside every fat little girl, there is a skinny little girl screaming to get out."

And I said, "Inside this fat little girl, there is a skinny little girl screaming, 'I'm hungry!' "

They sent me anyway. Camp To Ke Ro No. Camp Fat.

The first thing they tell you after they take away all your money so that you can't buy snacks even if they had a snack bar, the first thing they tell you is that being fat isn't healthy. Miss Coolidge, who is in charge of Camp Fat, also tells you that you'll like yourself much better if you're thin. I liked myself enough already. My trouble was that I especially liked myself well fed.

They had an assembly for the parents, too. Here Miss Coolidge told them how Camp Fat was going to make us lovely and healthy. They added the *lovely* for the parents. They showed slides of kids before and after camp. The whole program was like a long commercial for diet Pepsi, so l watched the audience; it was easy to see where a lot of baby fat comes from.

At the first weigh-in all you're allowed to wear is a towel. I took a very small one. It is more embarrassing, but it weighs less. If you've been fat as long as I have, you've learned a thing or two. Some kids who had been to Camp Fat for three years in a row didn't know that. My goal was to lose fifteen pounds in six weeks. That's a lot for a kid.

All of our counsellors were middle-aged and muscular except Miss Natasha. Miss Natasha came only at night; she came to our cabin only on Friday night. That first Friday, I had been lying in bed thinking that if they didn't put something chocolate on the menu soon, I was going to either foam at the mouth or kick the cook some place indecent, when this pinpoint of light came waving through the darkness. It stopped at Christy Long's bed. Christy had been crying again. And don't think that listening to her helped anything. Of course, Christy had two reasons to cry; she was supposed to stop sucking her thumb besides stop eating. Miss Coolidge had promised to work on the crying the next year.

Miss Natasha's light didn't stop at every bed. She came to mine right after Christy's. She introduced herself.

"That's a weird name," I said. "Really weird."

"It's Russian," she answered.

"Well, you guys sure didn't make it to the moon first," I said.

"You mean the moon moon?" she asked.

"Yeah, like up-in-the-sky moon. How come you don't know?"

"Oh," she said, "I don't think about things like that very much. I hardly think big at all. I think little."

"I thought that Miss Coolidge would want you to think thin."

"Oh, yes, that, too," she said. "That's why I'm here. To help you to think thin. Do you wish to have dialogue?"

"If it's chocolate covered and has three scoops of whipped cream," I answered.

"When I ask you if you wish to have dialogue, it means, do you wish to talk, back and forth, with me?"

"You want me to talk?"

"Yes. Tell me what you're thinking, and then I can tell you what I think of what you're thinking, and so on."

"First of all, I'm thinking that I would like to run a fever, a fever of about one hundred and eighteen degrees. They'd get me out of here pretty fast then."

Miss Natasha said, "I really thought that since you were awake, you would want to talk. Otherwise, I wouldn't have bothered to come tonight."

"What kind of dialogue did you have with Christy Long?" I asked. I didn't wait for Miss Natasha to answer because I wanted to tell her something else that I was thinking: "That Christy is one kid I'm sure going to show to my parents. She makes me look good. She's not only fat and sucks her thumb but she also cries a whole lot. The next one I'm going to show my mother is Linda Stark. She has pimples and picks her nose besides being fat." Miss Natasha didn't say anything, so I continued with some of that week's thinking. "Do you realize that the two Robins in our cabin weigh more than the three Lindas in Cabin Twelve? Robins! Their mothers should have named them Pelicans or Ostriches. Probably Pelican would be best because neither one of them can run worth a darn. Kim is the worst brat, though. She's only plump, so she acts like she's Miss Universe. She says that she has a glandular imbalance. Ha!" That was all I said to Miss Natasha. I had run out of dialogue.

Miss Natasha waited. When I didn't add anything else, she said, "Well, Clara, that's a start. Not an especially good one, but a start." And then she patted the blanket over my knee. As she did so, the ring that she wore on the little finger of her left hand, a plain looking gold dome ring, sprang open. I lifted her hand that had the ring, and it was the most beautiful watch I have ever seen.

Miss Natasha focussed her flashlight on it. The face of the watch was a thin layer of mother-of-pearl, and the numbers that weren't actual numbers were tiny jewelled flowers. That's why the lid was domed so that they wouldn't get mashed. The hands seemed to float to the proper time.

"Oh," I said, "I thought that that was just a plain old ring."

"Yes," Miss Natasha said. "It looks plain, but I made it open easily."

"You made it?"

"Yes, I made it. That was my work long ago."

"In Russia? I thought that Communists don't like fancy watches or people to wear them."

"When I lived in Russia, there was not only a shop for fancy things like this but also a very fancy king and queen who bought many of them."

"What was the matter with this one? Couldn't you sell it?"

"I never tried. I couldn't take the things that I made out of the country when I left. Except one thing. I made this watch in America."

"It sure doesn't look like what it is."

"Yes. It looks plain, but, you see, I made it open easily."

She was about to close the ring again when I asked her to give me another look. She held her hand close under my face and focussed the light on it again. I put my ear to it and heard the faintest whir. A tiny whir. "Is it a Swiss watch movement?" I asked.

"No, Timex," she laughed. And then she closed the top dome over the watch. Miss Natasha checked the other beds quickly but did not stop at any others. She must have gone on to the next cabin. I fell asleep right after she left.

We had to jog to breakfast every day. It was never anything worth running for. You just had to run—one of the rules. You would think that Camp Fat would be the cheapest camp in the nation. They spent practically nothing on food and absolutely nothing on chocolate.

We had to write home every Sunday.

Dear Mom and Dad,

This is number one letter and you are lucky I have the strength to write it.

Clara

At our first weekly weigh-in I had starved off fourteen pounds, but the scale said two. Liar. Even the kids who had lost more than average didn't get any reward. Like chocolate.

Miss Natasha didn't come again until the next Friday night. I guessed that that was her night for our cabin. I was figuring out how I could manage a convulsion while I was waiting in line at the next weigh-in. I had just decided that I would throw myself on the floor, jerk my arms and legs around and mutter "chocolate, chocolate," when I saw Miss Natasha's light. She stopped at Christy's bed again. Christy had made progress; now she cried silently and only sucked her thumb between meals. Miss Natasha stayed at Christy's bed a long time. Then she flashed her pinpoint of light on this bed and that on her way to me. Everyone was either asleep or pretending, so mine was the next bed she stopped at.

"Do you wish to have dialogue?" she asked.

"Only if it's about French fried potatoes or cheeseburgers," I answered.

Miss Natasha laughed and sat on the edge of my bed. She put her flashlight into her lap and her hands on either side and leaned back, stretching her neck.

"Where's your ring?" I asked.

"I chose not to wear it this evening," she said.

"That's too bad," I said. "I thought we could dialogue about it."

"Not tonight. Is there anything else you'd like to talk about?"

"Frozen custard," I answered.

"Well, goodnight then," Miss Natasha said. She leaned over as if she were going to kiss me.

"Don't you dare kiss me," I hissed. "My overweight is due to a severe disease which is extremely contagious. One kiss from me, and you'll be fat all the rest of your entire life."

"Really?"

"Yes," I told her. "The State Department is thinking of sending me to India and Biafra to kiss all the kids there to

fatten them up, but my mother and father are extremely prej-
udiced and besides, my dad is not sure that the trip is tax
deductible."

"Well," Miss Natasha said, "I was leaning over only to
straighten your pillow."

"You can do that," I said.

She didn't move.

"You may do it now," I said.

As she leaned over, I started saying, "At the moment
I am very busy making a list of people that I am very person-
ally going to kiss and give . . ." I noticed a locket dangling
from a chain around Miss Natasha's neck. The locket was
shaped like a teardrop and was no bigger than a Tootsie
Pop; on the front cover was a scene of children wearing
wreaths of flowers on their heads and dancing in a circle.
Miss Natasha leaned forward so that I could examine it
better. It looked like a locket, but I couldn't find any way to
open it.

"What's the matter with this thing? Is it some kind of
phony locket?" I asked.

"No," Miss Natasha said, "I don't make phony jewels. It
has had an accident. Look on the back of it."

I did. The whole back of the locket was cracked and
chipped. It must have been beautiful before it was broken. All
green and gold. "Can't it open at all now?" I asked.

"Yes, it can. But it is very difficult."

"Why don't you fix it?"

"I did the best I can."

I looked down at her hands and this time I noticed that
her knuckles were all swollen, and her fingers looked like

someone had once taken them off and reattached them at crazy angles. Funny that I hadn't noticed them when I had seen the ring. I guessed that I had been too busy looking at the ring. "You got arthritis or something?" I asked.

"Yes," she answered.

"Do you take aspirin for it? Aspirin is supposed to be good for the minor pains of arthritis and other stuff."

"I'm afraid that I'm beyond taking aspirin," Miss Natasha said. "If you care to try to get the locket open, I think that you'll find that it is worth the effort. I was furious when it was damaged, but then I realized that nothing was coming out of my fury, so I repaired it as best I could. There is something very beautiful about having this locket work in spite of its being hurt."

All the time that she was talking about being beautiful and hurt, I was trying to get it open. Miss Natasha had been leaning forward and holding her flashlight so that I could work it. "Did Christy see this?"

"Yes."

"Did she get it open?"

"No. She couldn't. I tried to help her, though. But she couldn't get it open yet."

"No wonder it's so hard for me. Her spit from sucking her thumb is probably all over it, making it icky for me." Most of the trouble, though, was that the repair work had hidden the hinge, and I couldn't find whichways it opened. Finally, I did. And it did.

"Those are the same tiny children pictured on the out-side," I said.

Miss Natasha smiled and nodded yes.

"Why they're jewelled and gorgeous enough to make every Barbie doll in the country want to puke from jealousy. Tiny princes and princesses no bigger than peeled pistachios."

"Can you find the ring, on the top of the maypole?" Miss Natasha asked.

I did.

"Pull it."

I did. The tiny, jewelled children started swinging around the pole, and chimes played a pretty tune.

"*Au Clair de la Lune,*" Miss Natasha said. "*In the Moonlight.* That's the name of the song. Doesn't that fit?" she asked looking out the window.

"I guess I would say that it does," I admitted. "Is this a Swiss movement?" I asked.

"No, Walt Disney," she laughed. Then she snapped closed the beautiful locket.

"It sure closes easier than it opens," I said.

"Most things do," she answered. And then Miss Natasha left my bed and left our cabin.

How they could expect all that fresh air and exercise to do anything but make me more hungry, I'll never know. At our next weigh-in, I had lost a total of five pounds. That's a lot for a kid, but according to them, I was just on schedule. Five pounds every two weeks.

We had to write home again:

Dear Mom and Dad,

I feel so nauseous all the time that I would throw up if I had anything to .

Clara

I thought that maybe Miss Natasha was coming on some other night of the week, too, and that I was missing her because I was so sleepy from starvation and exhaustion. I waited for her to appear on Tuesday, Wednesday and Thursday, but she didn't come. When she finally did come on Friday night, I asked her, "You sure don't do much work around here. Don't you think it would be cheaper for Miss Coolidge to have a record player playing 'think thin' under our pillows?"

"But a record player can't talk back," she said, "or show you this." Miss Natasha held out her hand. In it was the ugliest, smelliest looking blob that I had ever seen in my life. There were no words to describe it, so I said, "Yicchh."

She didn't say anything, so I asked, "Did you damage this one, too?"

"In a way, I did. I was trying to preserve what is in here. Inside here is the only thing that I was allowed to bring out of my country when I left. I should have known better than to think that adding layers of plastic could preserve all of my fine workmanship. A plain, simple but strong exterior would have been better."

"It stinks. It sure smells rotten. Is that Christy's spit?"

"No. Christy is still working on the locket. You see, the plastics that they had when I left my country were not nearly as refined as they are now. This is celluloid, and it is discolored by light, and it smells so bad because it once caught on fire. Well, actually, I tried to burn off the plastic, but I found that the whole thing was in danger of melting. There is nothing to do but to chip it away. Very carefully. A little bit at a time."

"Yicchh," I explained. Miss Natasha continued holding her blob. "I don't think that I want to bother with it," I added.

"Most people don't want to," she said.

"Are you sure that Christy's spit isn't on it?"

"I'm sure," she said. "It's messy to get all the way through to the good parts, but it's worth it."

"Why don't you peel away all the gunk by yourself?"

"It is very difficult for me."

"Because of your arthritis?"

"Partly. And partly because I am not always sure that it is worth the trouble."

"Hunh! You just told me that it was worth it. Just this minute you told me that."

"But, of course, I can tell you that because for you it is. You are young, and you will have almost your whole life to enjoy what you will find inside. I have none of that anymore."

"Do you mean that when I get to what is inside that," I said, pointing to her blob, "that you will give it to me? Is that what you mean when you say that I will have my whole life to enjoy it?"

"No. That isn't what I meant. What I have inside here is too valuable for me to give you. I can only let you see it. What do you think I am? A fairy godmother?"

"And what do you think I am? Your mother's helper, Cinderella? Do you expect me to do all that work just to get a look at what's inside?"

"That's what you expect of everyone you meet," she said. "You expect everyone to see what is inside all that fat of yours. And not everyone can take the time. But you can. You have the time."

"Well, I'm not about to do all the work," I told her.

"Even though you'll have the image of what is inside with you for all the rest of your life?"

At that point in the dialogue I zonked my head to one side on the pillow and pretended that I had suddenly fallen asleep. Miss Natasha picked up her blob and walked out. She didn't even bother flashing her light on the other beds. She sure didn't earn her pay, I thought. Dialoguing with only two kids in a whole cabin. One stupid Friday night a week.

I had lost three pounds at the next weigh-in. It was really three and one fourth, but Miss Coolidge said that ounces don't count. Miss Coolidge is as narrow-minded as her skinny hips.

Dear Mom and Dad,
    Next weekend is Parents Visiting Day. Don't expect a Miss America,
            Cordially,
            Clara

Well, my parents came to Parents Visiting Day. They always like to see if they are getting their money's worth. To show them how lucky they were to have me for a daughter, I showed them two Lindas and one of the Robins. Also Christy Long. I noticed Christy showing me to her mother.

I looked all over for Miss Natasha, but she wasn't there. I even bothered to ask Christy if she had seen her today, and Christy took her thumb out of her mouth long enough to say that she had not.

Some parents must have brought some kids some goodies, which the weigh-in the next Monday showed up. Miss Coolidge shook her narrow head, clicked her thin tongue and said to every single girl who didn't lose any weight or who didn't lose enough, "Did Santa Claus come to you early this year?" She said it to each one. Including Kim. Ha. Ha.

I waited up for Miss Natasha on Friday, and after she finished with Christy, I pretended that I was asleep. Who was she that she should think that I would wait up for her? She sat on the edge of my bed, and I noticed that she was holding her blob. It wasn't hard to notice; it stunk as bad as ever.

"Aren't you even going to ask if I want dialogue?"

"Don't you?"

"All I want to know is why you didn't show up on Parents Visiting Day."

"I'll show up when they have Parents Visiting *Night*."

"Do you still want me to peel that gunk for you?" I asked.

"No," she said, "I want you to peel it for you."

"Aha!" I said. "You mean that you've thought it over, and you are going to give it to me after all."

"I told you that I am no fairy godmother. I do want you to work on it. It is worth it. But you must believe that yourself."

"Will you help?" I asked.

"I've already helped as much as I can."

I picked up Miss Natasha's smelly old blob and began prodding it with my finger. "You know," I said, "you ought to bring the watch so that I can keep track of the time and you ought to bring the locket so that I can listen to it as I work on this."

"I'll bring them. I'm glad you like them so much. As a matter of fact, I have to go back to Christy's bed to get the locket. She's still working on it. Now you must start alone. I'll be back shortly."

"Why don't you just leave it in my little old shop here, ma'am. I'll give you a claim check, and I'll call you when it's done."

"Clara," Miss Natasha said, "if you had all day to do it, you'd put it off and put it off, and it would never get done."

So I began the gruesome job, letting my mind wander. Miss Natasha returned to my bed and watched me work a little while longer before she picked up her blob and walked out. I had gotten so interested in picking away at that mess that I forgot that she had the locket on when she had returned from Christy's bed. I was sorry that I missed another chance to see and hear it.

Dear Mom and Dad,
    Only three things make me sick anymore. Kim, all the push-ups over 15, and the goop they call boiled cabbage.
                            Fondly,
                            Clara

I had decided to be friendly; that's why I signed it *Fondly*.

Even the smell of Miss Natasha's burnt plastic ball didn't bother me anymore. Maybe because I was so close to the end and there wasn't much of it left. Maybe because Miss Natasha brought the ring and the locket now and that helped to take my mind off it.

I finished on the last Friday before I went home. The week before the plastic coat had gotten so thin that I was able to see what was inside. It was gold and the size of an airmail stamp. I peeled away the last of the plastic and saw that the gold was a tiny book whose cover was jewelled and locked.

"I'll bet it is a miniature Bible," I said.

Miss Natasha was as anxious as I was to get to it. "Open it! Open it!" she urged.

I did.

Oh,
my pretty

Oh,
my Clara

Oh,
my pretty

Oh,
my love.

"Oh. Ohhhhhhh! Oh. Ohhh," I repeated, which is not at all like me. "I know now that you are going to give it to me, after all. That *is* me. That's a thin Clara. You made it just for me, didn't you?" I looked up at Miss Natasha with grateful tears in my eyes, which is also not at all like me. "You put all that mess on it so that I would have to realize that I'm not plain on the outside like the watch and I'm not damaged like the locket. I'm fat and a little nasty and have to take all that off by myself so that people can see the beauty inside. I know now, dear Miss Natasha, that you are going to give me the tiny gold book, the greatest treasure of them all."

"No, I am not," Miss Natasha said. "I told you that I'm no fairy godmother. Make your own pictures." And with that, Miss Natasha took the book from me and left.

When my parents came to take me home from camp, I could tell that they were pleased with the way I looked, so I said, "I need new clothes. Nothing fits."

They had another assembly for parents to tell them about how they should help us by making only skinny suppers and by not having a lot of snacks except cottage cheese and carrots around the house. I looked for Miss Natasha at the assembly. I wanted to say a different goodbye to her. I couldn't find her.

After the assembly broke up, I separated from my parents and found Christy Long to ask her if she had seen Miss Natasha, and she hadn't either. There was nothing to do but to ask Miss Coolidge. I should have written my parents that Miss Coolidge was the fourth thing that made me sick. I thought

that my mother and father ought to meet Miss Natasha. And I
did owe her another goodbye, a better goodbye. I asked Miss
Coolidge if she had seen Miss Natasha.

"Miss Who?" she asked.

"Miss Natasha, the evening counsellor," I said.

"We have no Miss Natasha," Miss Coolidge said. "As a
matter of fact, we have no evening counsellor."

I looked at Miss Coolidge. She was skinny. Her legs were
skinny. Her elbows were skinny. Her brain was skinny. I
stared into her skinny eyes.

"Miss Natasha, you say?" she said. "Years ago, Camp To
Ke Ro No was an Arts and Crafts camp, and we had someone
here named Miss Natasha. She taught jewelry making. She
claimed that she used to work for the royal Russian court."

"Where do you think she is now?" I asked.

"Oh, she's dead. She died. As a matter of fact, it was after
she died that our arts and crafts enrollment went down so
badly that we had to change the camp. If Miss Natasha were
still with us, we never would have gone into the beef business."

It wasn't because Miss Coolidge called me beef that I
knew that I would never return to Camp Fat, and it wasn't
because she told me Miss Natasha was dead that I knew that I
would never return to Camp Fat. It was because of Miss Natasha that I knew that I would never *need* to.

Elizabeth Coatsworth

THE HORSE OF THE WAR GOD

THE BOY LIKED BEST tending the white horse in his shrine near the temple. All day the beautiful animal stood looking out through the pine trees towards the lake beyond, drowsing sometimes, and sometimes rousing himself to stamp his hoofs and switch his long tail. Then he would whinny in a long note that clanged like a trumpet through the temple grove and out across the roofs of the village, so that the villagers said, "The horse of the War God is calling to his master."

But when the boy came to the shrine with food and water for the white horse, and cloths to clean his glossy sides and combs to unravel the cascades of his mane and tail, the horse arched his neck down to his shoulder, and breathed softly against his face. No one except the horse loved the boy who was an orphan and a temple servant, and no one but the boy really loved the horse, though the villagers on their way to the temple of the War God stopped at his shrine to admire him and make their offerings.

And in fact so beautiful a steed could not be found in the length and breadth of the countryside. He was as white as the snow-covered crest of Fujiyama; his neck was as curved as a warrior's bow; and he was without blemish. If the God of War ever wished a worthy mount when he should ride out to meet the enemy, this was the animal.

But being a horse in a shrine is monotonous. It needed fortitude to endure the long hours when the rain drummed ceaselessly on the roof or the snow swept past the heavy open lattice of his dwelling. Then the boy would come slipping away from his other duties to bring his friend some special treat to make the day go quickly for them both.

He was a plain-looking boy, used to bearing heat and cold, used to harsh words and sometimes blows, used to wet garments and the feel of snow about his bare ankles. Since he had served the temple the priests had not been unkind to him. But to tell the truth they were a lazy lot, and more work fell on his shoulders than they were meant to bear. The head priest was an old man not fitted to serve the God of War. All his thoughts were on his garden and the etiquette of the tea ceremony. He never noticed that the tiles were beginning to fall from the temple roof like leaves from an old tree, nor that fewer and fewer of the villagers came to so run-down a temple. The other priests were shiftless and as long as their bowls were full of rice each day they did not care how the rats might carry away the offerings set on the tables before the god. Only the white horse in his separate shrine shone like a jewel in its case under the untiring care of the boy.

One day an elderly man came to the temple. For many years he had been away from his village. Now when he saw what had happened to the temple he was indignant. He had to speak out his mind to someone and as the boy happened to be the only one near, it was to him he spoke.

"This is a lamentable state of affairs indeed," he exclaimed. "When I was a young man this place was one of the most beautiful in Japan. People came from distant provinces to worship at the spot where the dragon died."

"What dragon, sir, may I venture to inquire?" asked the boy.

"Are you a temple servant and do not even know about the dragon?" cried the man. "Every village child used to know the story. Long ago on the bare mountain slope above this temple there lived a dragon which laid waste the countryside. Hero after hero went to fight with the monster but each left his bones to whiten the entrance of the dragon's cave. At last a young nobleman at the Emperor's court determined to take upon himself the quest. He was only sixteen years old, but he had a will like a sword, and would listen to no attempts to dissuade him. So, all in armour, he rode away towards this abode of death.

"But he was not alone. With him came a young girl, a lady-in-waiting at the court, who loved him, and insisted on sharing with him the dangers of the encounter. Surely now," said the villager, breaking off, "you remember the rest of the story?"

"No, honoured sir," said the boy, "I have never heard it before."

"Shame be to this temple and its priests, then!" said the old man. "When the young nobleman came near the entrance of the cave, he left the maiden with the horses in this grove of trees, while he went up to face the monster in its lair. Signs enough and to spare he found of its presence, but the dragon had retreated to the depths of its cave. No taunts could induce it to come forth, for it knew that in this boy's hand lay its appointed death.

"Now dragons are very fond of music, and when the girl heard her beloved in vain summoning the creature to battle, she remembered a flute she had brought with her to solace her companion on the way. So, drawing this from its case, she placed it to her lips. Although her heart was nearly bursting with terror she played on it so beautifully that the dragon forgot its forebodings and came out of the cavern to hear, and so fell before the young warrior's sword.

"But when the boy leaped down the hillside shouting out the news of his victory, he found all silent among the trees. His love was lying on the ground, her flute still in her hand. The struggle between her great courage and her great fear had been more than her slight body could bear, and with the last note of music, she had died. This temple was built to the God of War to commemorate the killing of the dragon. Oh, shame that this story should be told here as something strange and out-of-the-way!" And shaking his head the old man returned to the village.

Perhaps until then the boy had taken for granted the way things went at the temple. But now he saw everything with new eyes. Here a great deed had been enacted long ago and honoured in the building of these shrines. How wrong of the priests of to-day to allow the place to fall into disrepute! In a few years no one would come any more; the temple would be empty and ruined. Only the pine trees and the rocks of the steep mountainside would remember the young warrior's courage; only the wind would tell of the song the maiden had played.

Going about his tasks, the boy brooded over these things. He determined to speak to the head priest if he had the opportunity, and only a few days later the chance came. He had been ordered to clean out the pool which was overlooked by the small building where the priest invited his guests for tea. Fastening his garments high, the boy waded into the cold water with a broom of twigs, sweeping the rocks and hollows clean of the gathered silt. When all was shining he looked at his work, not quite satisfied. At last he broke off a branch of scarlet maple leaves—for it was autumn—and let it catch between two boulders.

"I see that in spite of your rough exterior you have the soul of an artist," said a voice behind him, and he turned to find that the head priest was standing near. "I suppose you are one of the temple servants? I think I have noticed you."

"The horse of the honourable War God is my especial charge," murmured the boy, bowing.

"You have shown a real sense of art in sweeping the pool," said the head priest.

This was the time to speak. Confused by his own daring, he said, almost in a whisper, "Pray forgive me. The temple, your honour must have noticed—the tiles! Ever since my insignificant arrival—how few people come! Matters grow worse and worse! So few offerings!"

But the head priest stopped him, raising one old hand.

"These matters disturb the tranquillity of my thoughts. I must suggest to you that you have behaved unsuitably in speaking to me in this manner." And without again glancing at the boy he disappeared within the shadows of the temple.

"Alas!" thought the other, gazing after him, "he is so old and gentle, he scarcely sees the world he lives in and cannot rouse himself to save us." And he took his disappointment to the shrine of the white horse.

A few nights later there arose a great storm. From behind the hill above the temple it poured. And with the wind came great torrents of rain that fell from the sky like cataracts, lit by flares of lightning, and resounding with thunder.

Restless was the sleep of the priests that night and no one dared so much as to open a door upon the mad world outside, except the boy, who slipped away and ran through the turmoil to join the white horse.

"I could not leave you alone," he whispered, "when all the demons of the storm are loose."

But the horse did not seem frightened. He nuzzled the boy's face, and then stood quietly, until at last the boy fell asleep, wet and cold as he was. But no sooner was he asleep than he heard a great voice calling:

"Come hither, horse! Come hither that I may ride!"

And looking up, he saw the white horse standing above him with raised head. The shrine doors had opened of themselves and outside he saw standing the dark form of the God of War himself, all in armour, the red lacquer of his face gleaming terribly in the flashes of lightning.

Then the boy prostrated himself, but above him he heard the white horse answer:

"And where shall we ride, O my master?"

And the God of War answered in a voice that mingled with the thunder above the sound of the increasing cataract of the rain:

"Against this temple of mine which has dishonoured me, shall we ride! And against this village which has forgotten me, shall we ride! And not one wall of this unworthy temple shall stand in the dawn, and not one man shall open his eyes upon the morning's sun!"

Then said the white horse:

"Shall no one be spared, O my master?"

And the War God cried:

"Not one shall be spared."

Then said the white horse:

"I will not come."

And at his words a silence seemed to come upon the tempest, a suspense that was broken only by the groaning of the trees.

Then the War God cried in a voice that shook the shrine:

"I will lash you with lightning! You shall feel the weight of my wrath like fire upon you! Once more I command you! Come forth!"

And the boy felt the horse trembling above him, but once more he said:

"I will not come, O my master."

Then the boy heard the rattle of the War God's armour, as he moved his arm, and he shrank waiting for what was to come. But instead of the consuming flame he expected, one more question pierced the storm:

"Why do you defy me?"

And the white horse answered:

"O my master, I defy you for the sake of love. There is one here who has served me since first we met, putting my need always before his own. It is for his sake that I have presumed to disobey you, and for his sake I yield up the life I have forfeited."

The night grew heavy with consideration, but at last the voice of the War God came:

"Obedience is a virtue. Gratitude is also a virtue. For this one time I will not demand that you choose between them. And for your sake I will spare this temple and this village, though I shall return unless they mend their ways, and as a proof I leave my mark upon their door."

And with that came a last crash and blaze of thunder and lightning outside, and afterwards the storm died away, and even the wind was silent and only the heavy rain-drops dripping from the trees remained to show what a flood had poured over them.

Then having embraced the knees of the white horse, the boy ran through the darkness and roused the priests, whom he found huddled together. He told them what he had seen and heard, and some were filled with awe and some scoffed and said he had been dreaming. But at dawn they found that the door of the temple itself had been struck by lightning, and the marvel was that there remained upon it a white scar shaped exactly like an arrow.

And seeing this, no one doubted the boy's story any longer. The old head priest resigned his office and retired into a life of contemplation, and the other priests set about repairing the temple they had so long neglected, and through all Japan the story spread until pilgrimages were made from the furthest provinces to behold the wonderful white horse who had turned the War God from his purpose, and the arrow-shaped mark of the lightning upon the temple door.

So between the offerings made by the pilgrims and the busy lives of the priests, the temple became more beautiful than it had ever been. In time the boy rose to be head priest, governing the affairs of the temple prudently and humbly, and never forgetting the love that bound him to the white horse, with whom he still spent long hours that made the days pass happily for them both.

Virginia Hamilton

THE YEAR
HALLOWEEN
HAPPENED
ONE DAY EARLY

*The scariest night of the year? That's Halloween. Halloween's the
last day—the thirty-first—of October. But in 1938 for Willie Bea,
her family, and six million other people, it happened one day early.*

THERE WAS A commotion downstairs. For a
minute Willie Bea couldn't tell what was going on.
Everybody was talking at the same time. She could
hear her father moving fast from the door to the couch. Then
something heavy fell on the couch and pushed the couch up
against the wall. Whoever had fallen was quick to get up
again because the springs of the couch squeaked the way they
would when someone got up from them fast after sitting down

on them hard. Willie Bea could tell that was what happened. It sounded like somebody was hurt bad or something, moaning and crying. It was a woman, sounding scared to death.

"What's the matter, what's happened?" they heard Willie Bea's mama say.

"You have an accident with the car?" they heard her papa ask.

"It's awe-fel! It's jus' aw-awe-fel!" they could hear the woman cry, in bitter anguish.

"What?" whispered Willie Bea.

The moaning, crying voice sounded familiar.

"What?" whispered Bay Sister.

"Shhhh!" said Willie Bea. Carefully, she crept farther down the stairs. She had Bay Sister by the hand and she knew Bay Sister would take Bay Brother's hand without her having to tell her. Someone always took Bay's hand on the dark staircase. It was a closed staircase, steep and without a banister. Going down, a person had to touch one of the walls or lean on one for balance. Willie Bea was leaning her shoulder into the wall on her right. They crept down the stairs and stopped again, hidden from sight behind the wall. Willie Bea stood on the final stair before the open landing, listening.

She decided whoever was upset in the living room would feel better once she saw their wonderful costumes—two ghosts and one hobo. . . .

"It's the end of ev-ree-thing!" the woman cried. "Oh, my lord in heaven, it's awe-fel, it's aw-awe-fel!" . . .

Willie Bea eased them down onto the landing. The landing was lighted by the glow from the living-room lamps. She pulled Bay Sister, who pulled Bay Brother, behind her. She wanted the three of them in their costumes to just sort of flow into view. Just to appear there, like Halloween phantoms.

"The Gobble-uns are here!" Willie Bea announced, in as good a voice as the announcer Don Ameche or that Harry Von Zell announcer. . . . They stood there, the three of them, as dressed up, as frightening as they could be.

No one heard Willie Bea. No one was listening. For the living room was a crazy, mixed-up scene. . . .

This tall, very good-looking man stood in the middle of the living room. Not her father. The man had on a great coat of dark wool. He'd unbuttoned the coat and flung it open. He had on a dark felt hat that matched the coat. Its crown was dented from front to back, with a stiff brim turned up slightly on the sides. Willie Bea glimpsed a gorgeous tuxedo suit of clothes under the man's coat. Suit jacket with satin lapels. A white dress shirt with gold-like buttons. There was a satin bow tie. The man had on a handsome gold chain draped across his chest. Willie Bea knew there would be a watch in the man's watch fob. The gent's shoes were white, and black on the shiny top front and the sides of the heels.

"Mr. Hollis, do sit down, won't you?" Willie Bea's mama was saying.

But the man, Mr. Hollis, couldn't sit down. For hanging on his shoulder, being held in an almost standing position, was wonderful Aunt Leah. . . . What in the world is she doing here? wondered Willie Bea.

Aunt Leah had on a full-length, to-the-floor, silky black, honest-to-goodness evening gown. It was the kind of evening dress that daringly bared the neck and the shoulders. It was the first evening gown Willie Bea had ever seen on anybody outside of the ladies in the movies. Aunt Leah had on a necklace of glistening pearls that came down to her waist and were tied in a pearly knot halfway down. She had on gold, low-cut dress shoes with very high heels. She wore a three-quarter-length, Norfolk-type, precious Persian fur coat that must have cost a fortune. . . .

Aunt Leah's hair was piled high on her head, with curls that cascaded down on each side at her temples. There was a black velvet bow ribbon pinned to her hair in the center, just above her forehead. A cluster of pearls decorated her earlobes. Her face was rouged and powdered to perfection. Willie Bea didn't know how any one person could be so perfectly beautiful in so many different ways as was Aunt Leah.

But now Aunt Leah was crying and moaning. Mr. Hollis supported her with one strong arm around her waist, inside that fabulous coat. There were no tears in Aunt Leah's eyes, although Willie Bea could see she was crying. But it was natural that Aunt Leah would dry-sob. It would never do to spoil that perfect, made-up face with real, salty tears.

Mr. Hollis half-carried Aunt Leah across to the radio. He rapidly turned the dial, trying to find something. You could hear garbled voices going in and out of hearing very quickly. Mr. Hollis took his fist and pounded the top of the radio.

"Now, here, don't do that!" said Willie Bea's father. He looked shocked. "That won't help anything. Tell me what you are looking for."

Mr. Hollis gave a glance around and down at Willie Bea's papa. He was that much taller. Willie Bea could tell he wasn't the kind of gent that took much direction or said quite a lot. There was mostly static on the radio now, after his pounding of it.

"Leah, sit down," Marva Mills said. "Won't you both sit down and tell us what is the matter?" She took her sister by the shoulder. But that made Aunt Leah hold on to Mr. Hollis all the more tightly.

"Oh, my lord above!" cried Aunt Leah.

"Leah, Mr. Hollis," said Willie Bea's papa, "please get hold. Do tell us."

"It's the world," said Mr. Hollis in a thin, tenor voice. "She call me after she heard it, but I already left to come for her."

Willie Bea was disappointed in the sound of Mr. Hollis. A gent his size should have a deep voice, rolling like thunder, she thought. What'd he say about the world?

"What?" Willie Bea's papa was saying. "The world? You mean there is war? It's the Nazis?"

"The world," murmured poor Aunt Leah. She clung to Mr. Hollis, eyes tightly closed. Her silk-stockinged legs seemed weak and trembly. "It's all over," she cried. "Heard it on the radio. The world. *The-world-is-coming-to-an-end!*"

Aunt Leah's legs buckled completely. Mr. Hollis lifted her off her feet and swung her tenderly up in his arms. It was then that Aunt Leah fainted dead away. . . .

There was silence in the living room, and a strong fragrance of roses. Just the sound of the radio, down very low with its static and its whistling. Willie Bea's papa had stopped fiddling with it. Not one station would come in clearly. Maybe it was just the Halloween night and witches messing up radios, Willie Bea thought fleetingly. But her better sense told her it was Mr. Hollis' pounding. Even she knew that something as magical as a radio with what they call its *sound waves* couldn't take that kind of battering. Shake everything up. Her father ran his hand rapidly through his hair a couple of times. Then he gave up on the radio, which he knew to have a weak tube, and turned back to the women on the couch. He stood there, lost in thought, staring at them.

"She comin' to now," Mr. Hollis said in his odd, high voice. He glanced from Aunt Leah to Willie Bea's papa. He was talking to Willie Bea's papa, the man of the house. "She'll tell you now. She comin' to."

A moment ago, Willie Bea and Bay and Bay Sister had crept into the room. All three of them squeezed into the overstuffed easy chair facing the couch, surrounded by the heady scent of roses. That was the fragrance of the smelling-salts mixture in the bottle that Willie Bea's mama waved under Aunt Leah's nose.

"Uh-nuh, uh-nuh," moaned Aunt Leah with each pass of the bottle. She came to in stages. Willie Bea watched each stage, her eyes fixed on Aunt Leah's perfectly made-up face. . . .

The first stage of coming to was an anguished look that contorted Aunt Leah's face. Willie Bea's mama had her arm around her sister. And when she saw Leah's strained expression, she gently massaged her shoulder.

After the look had passed and her features relaxed, Leah's eyebrows knitted together. Her lips parted and her fingers clutched at her evening gown. Willie Bea's mama put down the bottle of smelling salts and clasped one of Leah's hands in hers.

Aunt Leah's eyes fluttered wide open. She didn't look around, she looked straight into Willie Bea's face. She squeezed her sister's hand so hard that Willie Bea's mama winced.

"They've come. They landed," Aunt Leah said, straight at Willie Bea.

"What, Leah?" said Willie Bea's mama.

"Oh, it's awful!" said Aunt Leah, and she began to cry. Now real tears fell and marred the rouge on her cheeks. "Martians!" she said. "From the planet Mars! Landed right there in the state of New Jersey!"

"Now, Leah!" said Willie Bea's mother. She looked alarmed, but very doubtful.

"I'm tellin' you, I heard it on the radio," said Aunt Leah. "It was on the *radio*!"

They were silent at that. All of them. For if it came over the radio, if it was one of those sudden news bulletins, like urgent messages from on high, then it had to be true.

"Leah, are you sure?" said Willie Bea's papa. He stood before the couch, his hands deep in his pants pockets.

"Listen here," Aunt Leah said. She took her hand from her sister's and began to shape the air in front of her as she spoke. "This radio announcer," she began, "starts out sayin' that, incredible as it seems, some strange *beings* has landed in the New Jersey farmlands. And that they are the first of an *invading army* from the planet Mars!" Aunt Leah looked around at all of them.

They were speechless—Willie Bea's mama and her good papa. Staring at Aunt Leah, tongue-tied. It was too much for Leah to be making up, their looks seemed to say.

Willie Bea felt her heart leap into her mouth.

"Now a battle was fought," Aunt Leah continued. "The government sent our army of seven thousand men to fight this *monster machine* full of invaders out of Mars.

"Our army had rifles. They had machine guns!" Aunt Leah cried silently now, and when she could, she spoke again. "One hundred and twenty of our army soldiers survived. One hundred and twenty, *that's all*! And the rest, fallen all over the battlefield, some place called Grover Mill or somethin'. They were crushed and trampled by the monster. Burned to a cinder by the heat ray."

"Heat ray!" said Willie Bea's papa. He looked off then, gazing at the walls, as if some distant light had smacked him between the eyes.

"That just the beginning," Aunt Leah said. She paid no attention to the fact that her face and nose were streaming wet. But Mr. Hollis did. He leaned over and handed Willie Bea's mama his silk handkerchief. Marva took it and gently began dabbing at Leah's face. "It was awful," said Aunt Leah. "It went on and on. The announcer breaking in on the shows, don't you see? See, the Martians has plowed through the whole state of New Jersey. They goin' in *New York City*!" She paused and took a deep breath.

"Leah, could you be mistaken?" whispered Willie Bea's mama, as though she could hardly breathe.

"She heard it on the *radio*," Mr. Hollis said, and that was finally enough evidence to the truth of what Aunt Leah was telling them. For the bulletin flashes that came over the radio with news of the world were always true.

"And then the radio announcer standin' on the rooftop," said Aunt Leah. "Sayin' he seein' them Martians, tall as skyscrapers. They wade across this Hudson River into New York City. Said now they lift their metal hands!"

Ever so slowly, Aunt Leah's hands rose higher in the air. Willie Bea and Bay and Bay Sister were statues, stunned and tongue-tied.

"This is the end now, he said," said Aunt Leah. She stared at them earnestly. "He said, the announcer said, smoke comes out . . . black smoke, driftin' over the city. People in the streets see it now. Said they are running toward this East River, New York. Running away from it. Thousands of people dropping in the river like rats." Aunt Leah's shoulders shook. "Now the smoke spreadin' faster," Leah whispered. "It reaches the Time Square, New York City. People tryin' to get away, but it's no use! Said they're fallin' like flies. . . ."

As if in a dream, Willie Bea saw Aunt Leah's pearl necklace glisten and shimmer in the light. She was aware she was holding her breath a moment, for fear Aunt Leah would stop talking. Willie Bea had to know everything she could about the Martians. . . .

"The poor announcer," Aunt Leah moaned, holding her head as though it ached. "He one I usually listen to, I think. And he just shut off right then. He went dead on the air. The Martians and their machines just taken over everything. Oh. Oh! Who's to say they haven't already landed here?"

"Now, now," said Willie Bea's mama, patting Aunt Leah. She looked vaguely around at the windows, black with night. Then she noticed Willie Bea and Bay and Bay Sister right there in front of her. Her face lit up as if to say, How nice you all look! She didn't say it. But maybe they had reminded her. "It's a dark night out," she said to Aunt Leah. "It's the night for beggars all over town."

"After that, I didn't listen again," Aunt Leah went on. She didn't seem to have heard Willie Bea's mama. She sat up straight. Got hold of her black evening bag beside her and searched for her lipstick and powder puff. She sniffled and sighed. "I was 'most afraid to touch that radio. But I did. I turned it off, and it about burned my hand, too. But I pulled the plug! I'll *never* plug it in again! Then I called Avery." She nodded toward Mr. Hollis, but she did not turn her streaked face toward him. "That's all," she said. "I just wanted to come here, be with everybody." She smiled wanly. Her chin trembled. . . . "We'd better do somethin'!" she finished, and said no more.

Willie Bea's papa stood there, wondering what to do. "Don't have a telephone," he said absently. "If I did, I could put in a call to Officer Bogen downtown. And he could put in a call to the Xenia sheriff, although I don't know what good that would do." This last spoken to Mr. Hollis.

There was no telephone anywhere around. It was a long, dark mile into town.

"Don't understand clearly what this is all about," Jason Mills added.

Before anyone could say anything or do anything, the front door opened. It swung in ever so slowly, as if the black night had pressed too hard and had pushed it open. Willie Bea's papa jumped back and spun around, facing the door. Mr.

Hollis moved back on the piano bench and his elbows hit the piano keys. A great, discordant noise rose from the piano and spread around them. Willie Bea in the chair had her back to the door. She couldn't move. Neither could Bay Sister. But Bay Brother dived down into Willie Bea's lap. He scooted over, his face and head hidden under her arm.

Willie Bea shivered, thoughts paralyzed, as a stream of cold fell over the chair and down her neck.

"Hey, now, don't upset youselves. It just me." Uncle Jimmy's voice. Willie Bea went limp with relief.

She turned around to see Uncle Jimmy standing there, framed in the doorway. He had changed from his blue Sunday suit into his work overalls for doing his evening chores. He'd probably finished them, too. He had taken in their fright.

Uncle Jimmy glanced at the radio, then at his baby sister, Leah, all dressed up and fixing her face, streaked from crying. He noted the tall stranger sitting over there, and the way the gent carefully removed his elbows from the piano keys. The sound of the piano faded as Uncle Jimmy Wing framed in his mind the words he would later say to Aunt Lu: "Leah got herself a new dude." He had taken the scene in in a second, and understood it.

"I heard," he said, nodding at the radio. "Papa say, yall come on over home. Everybody there now but yall." He paused. He did not look directly at Willie Bea's papa or any-one. But Willie Bea felt that he was speaking directly to her papa, listening at him, figuring out how much her papa be-lieved.

Uncle Jimmy cleared his throat importantly. He looked up, gazing at the flowered wallpaper high above the couch.

"They seen them thangs lyin' low over by the Kelly farm," he said.

Suddenly, fear in the room was the shape of a poison-snake. Coiled. Rattles shaking.

"They gret big," Uncle Jimmy said, his voice low. "Gleamin' eyes," he said. "V-shaped mouths. Big as trees. Big as houses. Tall as a standpipe, I heard—eighty foot high. Over there at the Kelly farm, on the north of town." With that, he shrugged. Reached behind him. And held up his arm for them to see.

"Got my shotgun!" he exclaimed grimly, looking directly at Willie Bea's papa. There in his hand was his deadly shotgun. He knew Willie Bea's papa didn't own a gun, wouldn't have one in his house. Uncle Jimmy stepped out of the house onto the porch. "Yall come on over home," he said. "There mightn't be much time." He closed the door behind him.

There was something absolutely serious about the sight of Uncle Jimmy's shotgun. It stunned all of them there in the living room. Any doubt they might have had vanished. The snake of fear struck them hard.

"Oh, my lord above!" cried Aunt Leah. Getting to her feet, she spilled powder and lipstick on the floor. Mr. Hollis, halfway out of his seat, folded her in as she wrapped her arms around his neck.

Willie Bea's mama, always neat, bent to retrieve the make-up. Stuck it in Leah's purse. "I'm going over home," her mama said. She rushed out into the kitchen and came back with a modest tin of Halloween candy and her black everyday pocketbook.

"Marva," said Willie Bea's papa.

"You can stay here if you want to," Marva said.

"I didn't say that. Did I say that?" said her papa.

"No, but that's what you might be thinking, to stay," her mama said. She grabbed up Bay Brother, who was quite happy to be folded against her.

"Did I say what I was thinking?" her papa said. "I don't doubt what Leah and Jimmy have heard," he said, uncertainly.

"Willie Bea, come on. Bay Sis," said her mama.

"Can we trick-and-treat now?" Bay Sister asked.

"Trick-and-treat over home," Willie Bea's mama said.

Willie Bea's mama was on her way out of the door. She turned back. "Leah? Stop that in front of the children!" Aunt Leah was being comforted tightly by Mr. Hollis. The next moment Mr. Hollis was threading his way around Willie Bea, Bay Sister and their papa, leading Aunt Leah out of the house. They were outside, and Willie Bea and Bay Sister were right behind them.

Willie Bea's papa was left. He might make his way over home. He could walk downtown. It would take him no more than fifteen minutes at the most. Time passed while Jason Mills decided what to do.

He turned up the radio. Stations came in and out. There was static. He didn't hear a thing that sounded like a news flash. And if there had been a catastrophe, wouldn't the news have been on every station on the radio? Just the way the horrible destruction of the *Hindenburg* dirigible had been all over the radio last year?

The *Hindenburg* had been an 800-foot, cigar-shaped super-balloon that was steered and fueled by hydrogen fuel. A radio newsman had been right there a year ago, routinely announcing the return of the *Hindenburg*. It had crossed the ocean from Germany many times before. It carried ninety-seven passengers. And, tragically, it had caught fire as it approached its Lakehurst, New Jersey, mooring.

New Jersey again!

Thirty-five passengers had been killed; and in half a minute the great dirigible was a twisted heap of steaming, molten metal.

Heat. A heat ray, wasn't it, Leah had said?

The Germans, too! They had made the *Hindenburg* and other great dirigibles they called zeppelins. Ingenious Germans!

Hindenburg! The man Von Hindenburg, President of the German Republic, had submitted to Nazi power. He had named Adolf Hitler Chancellor of Germany in 1933. The fascist Hitler!

Jason checked his pocket watch. After nine. The night wore on.

But Germany, the *Hindenburg*, an old catastrophe. New Jersey again and a new catastrophe.

Could it be . . . ? An invasion not from Mars. No indeed, not. But from Germany? Von Hindenburg. Nazis. The fascist power on the move!

Jason Mills turned off the radio, turned out all but one light. He gathered money, keys, a warm sweater, which he put on under his overcoat, and left the house. He didn't think to lock the door until he was down the front steps. He went back up, back into the house. He went into the dining room. No one had thought to blow out the candle in the sweet pumpkin on the dining-room table. He did so. He went into the kitchen and locked the back door. Then he came through the house again.

He went to the closet in the dining room and got Marva's winter coat for her. He remembered she had gone over home without even a sweater over her dress. Next he went to the sideboard and got the life-insurance policy out of his business drawer. No telling what might happen this night. He took his bankbook, too, although there was never much money in his account. Then he went out, locking the front door behind him. There had not been a reason to lock up the house for some time. The family had not been far from home in so long.

He went quickly to the Dayton road and crossed it, going over home. They'd all be talking, over home. Someone— maybe him—would speak about organizing a patrol for this end of town. Or whether they should leave the area. There certainly were enough autos in the family to transport them all. But where would they go? He wouldn't have a gun. Perhaps his axe would do.

Jason Mills strode away in the Gobble-un dark. The huge field pumpkin was left glowing on the front porch. Its pyramid eyes gleamed wickedly. Its light was orange, flickering, gathering in the night.

All over town, in other towns, in cities, the Martians landed. And everywhere, fearing for their lives, the people panicked.

Across the country, jack-o'-lanterns guarded porches. Their gap-toothed grins were scornful. Somewhere, deep a-pumpkin, they laughed in silent, mocking shrieks.

• • •

Later, of course, everybody discovered it was all a mistake. The October 30 attack was a War of the Worlds *radio drama*, the unstoppable Martians a figment of writer H. G. Wells's imagination.

It hardly seemed funny when it was happening. But as time mellowed people's memories, they began looking back at 1938, with a chuckle, and speaking of it as the year Halloween happened one day early.

(Note: "The Year Halloween Happened One Day Early" is taken from Chapters 7 and 8 of *Willie Bea and the Time the Martians Landed*.)

ABOUT
THE AUTHORS

ARTHUR BOWIE CHRISMAN 1889–1953

Arthur Bowie Chrisman was born near White Post, Virginia. After attending Virginia Polytechnic Institute for two years, he worked as a schoolteacher, farmer, draftsman, movie extra, and writer. A noted raconteur, with a strong interest in the Orient, he was awarded the Newbery Medal for *Shen of the Sea* (1926), an edifying collection of stories designed to illuminate aspects of Chinese history or culture. Our selection, "Ah Tcha the Sleeper," was taken from this book.

BEVERLY CLEARY 1916–

Beverly Cleary was born in McMinnville, Oregon. She graduated from the University of California at Berkeley and received a degree in librarianship from the University of Washington in Seattle. In 1940 she married Clarence Cleary, and they have two children.

Before turning to writing full time in 1950, Mrs. Cleary was a children's librarian. She is the author of more than thirty books for young people. *Ramona the Brave* was a Newbery Honor book in 1978, and *Dear Mr. Henshaw* was awarded the Newbery Medal in 1983.

Dear Mr. Henshaw was Mrs. Cleary's response to many requests for a book about children of divorce. Writing in *The New York Times*, Natalie Babbitt said, "Beverly Cleary has written many very good books. . . . This is one of the best. It is a first-rate, poignant story. . . . There is so much in it, all presented so simply that it's hard to find a way to do it justice."

"The Baddest Witch in the World" is a chapter from *Ramona the Pest,* her anecdotal novel of 1968.

ELIZABETH COATSWORTH 1893–1986

Elizabeth Coatsworth was born in Buffalo, New York, graduated from Vassar, received her M.A. from Columbia, and married Henry Beston, a writer. A longtime resident of Nobleboro, Maine, she won the Newbery Medal in 1931 for

The Cat Who Went to Heaven. Her vivid imagination shines through works like *You Say You Saw a Camel?* (1958), *Lonely Maria* (1960), *The Princess and the Lion* (1963), *Marra's World* (1975), *The Werefox* (1975), *Snow Parlor and Her Bedtime Stories* (1972), *They Walk in the Night* (1969), and *All-of-a-Sudden Susan* (1974). One of our Coatsworth selections, "The Horse of the War God," comes from *Cricket and the Emperor's Son* (1932), her collection of Japanese fables, while the other, "Witch Girl," comes from a 1953 issue of *Story Parade*.

ELEANOR ESTES 1906–1988

Eleanor Estes was born in West Haven, Connecticut. She was educated at the Pratt Institute. She married Rice Estes in 1932, and they had one child.

Mrs. Estes had a career as a librarian before turning to writing full time in 1940. She was awarded the Newbery Medal in 1952 for *Ginger Pye* and is particularly noted for her authentic accounts of childhood experiences, that can be found in such marvelous collections as *The Moffats* (1941), from which our selection, "The Ghost in the Attic," was taken; *The Middle Moffat* (a Newbery Honor Book in 1943); *Rufus M.* (a Newbery Honor Book in 1944); *The Hundred Dresses* (a Newbery Honor Book in 1945); and *The Moffat Museum* (1983).

CHARLES J. FINGER 1869/71[?]–1941

Charles J. Finger was born in Sussex, England, immigrated to the U.S. in 1887, and became a citizen in 1896. He had held jobs with the railroad; served as a music school director; and worked as a magazine editor. A frequent traveler, he won the Newbery Medal in 1925 for *Tales from Silver Lands*, a collection of South American fantasies, from which our selection, "The Magic Ball," was taken. He was the author of more than sixty books of adventure and biography, including *Travels of Marco Polo* (1924), *Tales Worth Telling* (1927), *Adventure Under Sapphire Skies* (1931), and *Golden Tales of Faraway* (1940).

PAUL FLEISCHMAN 1952–

A second-generation children's writer, Paul Fleischman was born in Monterey, California. He attended the University of California at Berkeley and the University of New Mexico. He married Becky Mojica, a nurse, in 1978.

He is an excellent stylist who utilizes a wide variety of geographical settings. His *Graven Images: Three Stories* (1982), from which our selection, "The Man of Influence," was taken, was a Newbery Honor Book in 1983. A collection of insect poems, *Joyful Noise: Poems for Two Voices*, won the Newbery Medal in 1989.

VIRGINIA HAMILTON 1936–

Virginia Hamilton was born in Yellow Springs, Ohio; attended Antioch College, Ohio State, and the New School for Social Research; and married Arnold Adoff, an anthologist and author. She won the Newbery Medal in 1975 for *M.C. Higgins the Great*. One of the most honored of contemporary children's writers, she has won the Edgar Allan Poe Award of the Mystery Writers of America (1974) and the National Book Award (1975). Her always entertaining books include *The House of Dies Drear* (1968), which was made into a film; *The Time-Ago Tales of Jahdu* (1969); *The Planet of Junior Brown* (a Newbery Honor Book in 1972); *Willie Bea and the Time the Martians Landed* (1983), from which our selection, the excerpt "The Year Halloween Happened One Day Early," was taken; *Sweet Whispers, Brother Rush* (a Newbery Honor Book in 1983); and her fantasy collection, *The Dark Way* (1990).

E. L. KONIGSBURG 1930–

E. L. Konigsburg was born in New York City. She graduated from Carnegie Mellon University and did graduate work at the University of Pittsburgh. In 1952 she married David Konigsburg. They have three children.

Mrs. Konigsburg has been a teacher as well as a writer. Our first selection, "A Halloween to Remember," was taken from her anecdotal novel *Jennifer, Hecate, Macbeth, William McKinley, and Me, Elizabeth*, a Newbery Honor Book in 1967.

In 1968, she won the Newbery Medal for *From the Mixed-up Files of Mrs. Basil E. Frankweiler*. Our second selection, "Camp Fat," was taken from her collection *Altogether, One at a Time* (1971).

MADELEINE L'ENGLE 1918–

Madeleine L'Engle was born on November 29, 1918, in New York City. She graduated with honors from Smith College and did graduate study at Columbia University. In 1946 she married Hugh Franklin. They have three children.

Madeleine L'Engle has been active in the theater in addition to writing books. She won the Newbery Medal in 1963 for *A Wrinkle in Time*; *A Swiftly Tilting Planet* was named a Newbery Honor Book in 1981.

Of *A Wrinkle in Time*, *The Horn Book* wrote "[The book] makes unusual demands on the imagination, but it consequently gives great rewards." *The New York Times* said, "Madeleine L'Engle mixes classical theology, contemporary family life, and futuristic science fiction to make a completely convincing tale."

Our selection, "Poor Little Saturday," one of her few short stories, first appeared in the October 1956 issue of *Fantastic Universe*, a science fiction magazine.

PHYLLIS REYNOLDS NAYLOR 1933–

Phyllis Reynolds Naylor was born in Anderson, Indiana, and graduated from Joliet Junior College and American University. She has three children and her second husband, Rex V. Naylor, is a speech pathologist. Before turning to full-time writing in 1960, she worked as a teacher and magazine editor. Since then she has produced more than sixty books of fiction and nonfiction for adults and children, receiving the Newbery Medal in 1992 for *Shiloh*.

One of her favorite subjects is witches. Her novels include *Witch's Sister* (1975), *Witch Water* (1977), *The Witch Herself* (1978), *The Witch's Eye* (1990), *Witch Weed* (1991), *The Witch Returns* (1992). Our selection, "The Witch's Eye," is an extract from the book of the same name.

ABOUT
THE EDITORS

MARTIN H. GREENBERG has more than three hundred anthologies to his credit, including several prepared especially for children and young adults. His first trade anthology, *Run to Starlight: Sports Through Science Fiction*, was published by Delacorte Press in 1975. He is a professor of political science and literature at the University of Wisconsin.

Mr. Greenberg lives with his wife and young daughter in Green Bay, Wisconsin.

CHARLES G. WAUGH is a leading authority on science fiction, fantasy, and popular fiction in general. With Martin H. Greenberg and others, he has edited more than one hundred fifty anthologies in a variety of genres, including many for children and young adults. He is a professor of communications and psychology at the University of Maine at Augusta.

Charles Waugh lives with his wife and son in Winthrop, Maine.